PIROUETTES ON A POSTAGE STAMP
BOHUMIL HRABAL

AN INTERVIEW-NOVEL WITH QUESTIONS ASKED
AND ANSWERS RECORDED BY LÁSZLÓ SZIGETI
TRANSLATED, WITH AN INTRODUCTION
AND NOTES, BY DAVID SHORT

Pirouettes
on a Postage Stamp
Bohumil Hrabal

Charles University Prague
Karolinum Press 2008

*I withdraw everything that I have ever said
that was just to avoid my soul's damnation,
to which I still don't have the key.*
Bohumil Hrabal

ISBN 978-80-246-1447-2

BOHUMIL HRABAL (1914–97), the cat-loving, football-crazy, only semi-reconstructed beatnik, is gradually becoming familiar to the English-speaking reader,[1] as the author of bizarre (he would say, in many cases, grotesque) tales based on observation of everyday events and as the source of a number of screenplays.[2] Additional momentary notoriety accompanied the appropriately bizarre manner of his death – from falling out of his hospital window as he fed the pigeons.

Life, including the author's own, is at the heart of all his works. Thus many contain autobiographical elements, though it is not always possible to disengage them from the imaginative overlay. The present volume is unique amongst the works of Bohumil Hrabal in being overtly (auto-)biographical and, particularly, auto-philosophical. Its uniqueness also stems from its genre (he originally called it an 'interview-novel'; the 1996 Collected Works edition calls it merely a 'conversation', or 'dialogue'[3]) and from its being, in a sense, jointly authored (a feature which, though for different reasons and in different ways, it shares with *toto město je ve společné péči obyvatel*[4]).

Both the genre and the joint authorship make the present book reminiscent of Karel Čapek's *Hovory s TGM*:[5] each is a cooperative effort between a 'celebrity' (the writer Hrabal and Czechoslovakia's first president T. G. Masaryk) and a recorder of their thoughts (the Slovak-Hungarian journalist László Szigeti and the writer Karel Čapek respectively). One difference is that while in each case it is the writer who appears as titular author, in Hrabal's he is the 'celebrity', while Čapek is the recorder. This itself is curious, and adds to the book's uniqueness in Hrabal's oeuvre, since, as he repeatedly maintains, here and elsewhere, he saw his own role to be that of a recorder, not writer. One 'creative' similarity[6] between the two is that just as Čapek pruned and edited the text several times, after Masaryk had made his amendments to the draft typescript,[7] so too Hrabal's thoughts, at first reading apparently verbatim, as if lifted straight from the tape-recording, were actually heavily edited (with omissions and some juggling) by Hrabal himself after he had seen Szigeti's second version of the transcript (the full process is described in 'PS 1' in the original).[8] In this respect *Pirouettes* is like most of his other works: he was notorious for, indeed made a virtue or principle of, cutting and reorganising his texts several times over, a practice to which he inevitably alludes in this conversation.

Since the text nevertheless retains the character of a more or less verbatim oral record, it is occasionally awkward to translate, being full of false starts, anacolutha, and thematic and syntactic digression; the latter would be doubtless included, with pride, among the author's 'pirouettes on a postage stamp'. The text is also very uneven in the way Hrabal's oral discourse (in contrast to the more earnest Szigeti) is marked by code-switching (between an informal standard Czech and hypercolloquial forms – words and grammatical forms – more appropriate to Common Czech). And it is occasionally idiosyncratic in its vocabulary: no other late twentieth-century writer makes such regular use of the word *ludibrionism*, which will be seen to mean more than an indulgence in the *ludibrious* (which English dictionaries do recognise). The translation seeks to preserve as many of these characteristics as possible, so that it should still read as fairly informal, rather than having been beautified by editorial intervention. The original printed text is, however, particularly idiosyncratic in the use of punctuation and in this case I have, conversely, felt at liberty to do some minor reorganization here and there.

Hrabal's language generally is quite accessible. Apart from *ludibrionism*, the one Hrabalesque word *par excellence* is *pábení*, here left untranslated (though previous translators have used *palavering*). And a slight problem attaches to the title of the book – *Kličky na kapesníku* in the original. *Kličky* is a plural word referring to the bobs and weaves and tight manoeuvres that make up tackling and dribbling on the football pitch; as a plural form it carries with it the option of being used in the singular, as it occasionally is in the book. I have favoured the translation 'pirouette(s)', since that likewise refers to a motion of the whole body, and has been deemed appropriate enough by those who remember the footwork of the Hungarian footballer who first inspired the image for Hrabal; the expression is also not unknown in English football

9

journalism. (The 'postage stamp' of the translation replaces the 'handkerchief' of the original title as a more familiar English image of a confined space, and 'Pirouettes on a postage stamp' preserves the alliteration of the original title.) The literal sense of *klička* as 'loop' is, to the Czech mind, also associated with 'bow', or 'knot', hence when collocated with 'handkerchief' it may hint at the knots traditionally tied in handkerchiefs as an aide-mémoire – not inappropriate in a book consisting in the main of memoirs, though this other layer of meaning has not proved possible to conserve in the title of the translation.

The English-speaking reader might occasionally be thwarted by his ignorance of Czech literature, to which, unsurprisingly, Hrabal makes frequent reference. For that reason I have introduced footnotes, as economically as possible, to provide the minimum necessary background. I have used my judgement over the provision of sundry other footnotes, usually called forth by the need to explain some or other detail of Czech or Central European or other *realia* or cultural references that may be less familiar to at least some Anglo-Saxon readers. If it were thought that footnotes have no place anyway in a work which carries a subtitle containing the word 'novel', I would defend the practice on the grounds that, notwithstanding its literary form, unusual as it is, the work is none the less (auto-)biography and so non-fiction, and while readers of the original may have needed less editorial assistance, the reader from outside the Czech environment, especially one previously unacquainted with Hrabal, almost certainly does.[9] Similar grounds have led me to provide an index of names and of literary and other works mentioned. For the reader with a prior interest in Hrabal, the latter should aid the search for some background to quite a number of his other works. This unique, and uniquely processed, biographical record should help any future readers of Hrabal in translation to gain a better understanding of the man and his philosophy. The text is a complete rendering of the first regularly published edition, minus two of the three postscripts ('PS 2' and 'PS 3' are also omitted from the text of the Collected Works edition[10]), despite their provision of some additional background on the work's genesis.

Most important here is the light the postscripts throw on the work's occasionally transparent Hungarian focus; if less well known in the Anglo-Saxon world, Hrabal was and is extremely popular in Hungary, and it was a Czechoslovak-Hungarian journalist who conceived the format of the book as a means to enhance further the Hungarian reading public's familiarity with an already familiar author. A previous Hungarian accolade, and a kind of *quid pro quo* for Hrabal's own acknowledged debt to the Hungarian playwright and short-story writer István Örkény, came with the publication of a book in which Hrabal's name figured in the title, namely Péter Esterházy's *Hrabal Könyve* (Budapest, 1990 – the very year in which *Pirouettes* appeared in regular printed form); this has appeared in English, as *The Book of Hrabal* (Budapest, London, 1993; trans. Judith Sollosy). It is a rambling novel in which the lives of a young intellectual couple are (over-)shadowed by two members of the Hungarian security services in the guise of somewhat Rushdiesque 'angels'; Hrabal, or his spirit, is the sounding-board or prop that helps the woman in particular, who is pregnant and in two minds as to whether to have an abortion, to retain her sanity.

Finally, it should be borne constantly in mind that the text arose before the 'Velvet Revolution' (the conversations took place in 1984–85). Thus any references of the 'here' and 'now' kind, such as the comments on the politics of publishing, apply to conditions in the Czechoslovak Socialist Republic (1960–89).

David Short *Windsor, January 2007*

---

[1] For works previously translated see Miroslav Červenka *et al.*: *Sebrané spisy Bohumila Hrabala, vol. 19, Bibliografie, dodatky rejstříky*, Prague, 1997, pp. 276–78.

[2] Perhaps the best known films are *Cutting it Short* and *Closely Watched Trains*, though there have been others; some have been given an airing on British television, though well outside peak viewing times. A complete filmography is to be found in ibid. pp. 344–51).

[3] The 'original' sub-title applies to the first regularly published book edition (Prague: Práce, 1990). This was in fact preceded by a photocopied (samizdat) edition of thirteen copies taken from an amended typescript (Prague, 1987), of which the (deleted) sub-title had been *Rozhovory do autu* (approx. 'Conversations across the touchline', or '... out of play' – a football metaphor). The Collected Works sub-title is, then, a compromise return to the original one, but totally lacking the sporting allusion of either of its predecessors. The text is there not merely described as a dialogue, but is fully type-set as one, with the alternating speakers given throughout, as in a play; the names are typeset as capitals, Szigeti's questions in italics. (See *Sebrané spisy Bohumila Hrabala*, Vol. 17 [ed. V. Gardavský, C. Poeta and V. Kadlec], Prague, 1996, pp. [5]–126.)

[4] 'this town is in the joint care of its inhabitants' (the non-capitalisation of the first word of the title is deliberate). See my essay 'Bohumil Hrabal and Fun with Montage: Aspects of *toto město je ve společné péči obyvatel*', in *Bohumil Hrabal (1914–97): Papers from a Symposium* (ed. DS), London, 2004, pp. 59–81.

[5] See 'Linguistic authenticity in Karel Čapek's *Conversations with TGM*', in David Short: *Essays in Czech and Slovak Language and Literature* (London,

1996, pp. 31–49). The opening paragraphs include due reference to the pre-history of the genre, as represented notably by Plato and Goethe. The change of the present work's sub-title to 'dialogue' or 'conversation' is not without relevance here.

[6] There is also a *structural* similarity, in the inclusion of photographs, of Masaryk and Hrabal respectively. In *Pirouettes* these were by Tibor Hrapka, though they are not reproduced in the present version. They were the subject of 'PS 2', one of three 'appendices' to the original work; in it, Hrabal writes at length of this photographer's art as being like his own, a method of observing, cutting, selecting, rejecting, and he is plainly pleased with the outcome. Amongst other things he says: 'Tibor Hrapka often caught me in situations where I could not match up to my own photo, and where his photographs also had an extra half-dimension because in my civilian existence I [...] very much want to be as in a photograph... / For all that, Tibor Hrapka did capture me in several shots when I didn't know they were being taken, and so my mask, thanks to the alertness and artistry of the photographer, was remoulded into a human face.'

[7] See Čapek, *Čtení o TGM* (Prague, 1969).

[8] Hrabal might well have found this parallel, with both Čapek as fellow-writer and Masaryk as the celebrity in this type of Platonic dialogue, flattering – despite the ideological differences between them. Čapek's standing as a writer and gentleman is at least recognized in *Pirouettes*; Masaryk is mentioned just once, and then not by name, and only in the Čapek context. It is not inconceivable that Hrabal may have aspired to the standing with the readership (if not the establishment) of his own day that Čapek enjoyed in his and went along with Szigeti's project more willingly than his sometimes morose nature, and his avowed avoidance of fellow-writers, might suggest. His initial failure to win the approval of the (Communist) establishment for this book is apparent from the tenor of the anonymous reader's comments in the appraisal rejecting it on behalf of Československý spisovatel (see the 'Commentary' on the text in the Collected Works edition, p. 377).

[9] I have thought from the outset that an edited Czech edition of the work would not come amiss; the book has plenty of allusions which must escape the Czech reader, not to mention Hrabal's occasional factual slips, which might well go unremarked; I have sought to rectify those that I have identified.

[10] 'PS 2' is included in Vol.18 of the Collected Works under its sub-title 'Mask and Face'; 'PS 3' is reproduced in the Collected Works edition of *Pirouettes*, but only as part of the critical apparatus (pp. 378–80).

Mr Hrabal, when did you actually enter the world of books and literature?

The first book I ever had was an ABC. After I learned to read I was given an odd sort of book called *Master Naughty Grows Up*.[1] It was a story about a repulsive, wicked little boy who finally grew up to be a good boy. I saw myself not as the good boy, but as Master Naughty; I must have liked the book though, because I've still got it at home. Nobody else read it, just me, and now it's all fallen apart.

And who wrote Master Naughty?

Some Czech writer. It was just an ordinary children's book, with pictures. But I was even more fascinated by Bible stories. Bible stories, from Adam and Eve right through to the birth of Christ and the

---

[1] Anon: *Z ledajáčka ledaják. Veselé, zároveň však poučné vypravování o ledajákovi Ivánkovi* (Master Naughty Grows Up. A jolly but improving tale about naughty little Ivan). Prague, 1915. Unpaginated (32p.). A large-format (in excess of A4) children's book with lots of pictures. The title is slightly misleading in that while baby naughty Ivan grows up first into big naughty Ivan, he is, finally, after many improbable and supernatural adventures involving a car-ride with a baron, a bizarre flight in a balloon and his rescue by a bunch of dwarfs, much improved; having politely thanked the dwarfs he returns home never to annoy his parents again.

conversion of Saul to Paul. I learned those stories by heart. And the third book that made me what I am was Sokol-Tůma's *From the Mills of Bohemia*,[2] tales about country-folk, life at the water-mill and in the village generally, and it was all so amazing. And of course, later on I read crime fiction – Leon Clifton, Nick Carter, or cowboy books – Buffalo Bill, Wild Bill Hickock and the rest. When I was in about the fifth grade, I was given a book by Florence Montgomery called *Misunderstood*.[3] It's an unbelievably awful book, and most certainly not for children, because

[2] Hrabal is mistaken at this point: the highly popular *Z českých mlýnů* referred to here is not by the moralizing, patriotic, anti-clerical and antisemitic František Sokol-Tůma (real name František Tůma, 1855–1925), one of numerous nineteenth- and early twentieth-century Czech writers of conventional prose, also a playwright and journalist; it is in fact by Karel Tůma (1843–1917), a leading journalist (and long-term editor of Národní listy) and politician (MP for the National Party of Free-Thinkers). These humoresques, based on rural life and centred on the village mill, came out in numerous printings up to a total of eight volumes (1892–1917); a film was also made.

[3] Florence Montgomery (1843–1923), Victorian novelist, author of books for and about children, daughter of Admiral Sir Alexander Montgomery, 3rd Bt. The long (300p.) moral tale *Misunderstood* (1869) was extremely popular, despite being 'unbelievably awful': at least twenty-one editions appeared with Montgomery's original publisher (Bentley) up to 1887, with several more from MacMillan up to 1913, further English editions in the USA and Germany, and translations into several other languages, including Italian, Slovak (*Neporozumený*, trans. Margita Paulíny-Tóthová [1873–1948]) and Czech. The publishing history in Czech is not without interest, since its Victorian morality was obviously found 'useful' not only in pre-World War I Austro-Czech conditons, but was still felt worth republishing in pre-World War II Czechoslovakia, long after the last English edition. It first appeared, translated by Josefa Božena Koppová (d. 1917) under the title *Nepochopen* (1897) as a supplement to the Prague daily *Národní listy*. It was then retranslated ('from the 24th English edition') under the same title by Malvina Nekvindová-Nešporová (??–??) and published in book form in 1906; further editions appeared in 1916 and 1930. It is perhaps safe to assume that the wartime edition of the second translation was the version presented to Hrabal.

Humphrey, he's forever misunderstood, even in his own family. I never read the book to the end, it always made me so sad. Today I realize that I too was a bit misunderstood, actually like most children; it hadn't been a mistake when they gave me it, but the book had a higher purpose that I've only learned to appreciate since. Although I've got the book, I still haven't dared to finish it, so the boy Humphrey lives on like me. It was only last year that I learned that my hero had almost drowned. That's right. But they dragged him from the water along with his little brother, who wasn't hurt, though Humphrey injured himself so badly falling out of a tree that he was crippled for life – and lost the will to live. Which is why he died so young.

So you were magically drawn to mischief. But what mischief did you find in the Bible stories or the Tůma book?

I was permanently drawn to the unfolding tales. They're sort of miniature short-stories. In those days we had RE at school, and I was amazed at these abridged versions of great events...

And stories. But what did you get from those books in the way of ideas?

Nothing at all. Fun. I've always treated literature as fun as well. One Christmas my uncle gave me a book by François Rabelais, *Gargantua and Pantagruel*, a Renaissance work. It's some nine hundred pages of very funny and highly intellectual narrative, larded with quotations from the ancient Greeks and Romans. And that's where I really learned *and* understood what quotation is about: simply being an educationist and appealing to all the beautiful and meaningful things the past has to offer.

I expect you were taken by the work's ethical novelty, the creed of ethics of Gargantua and Pantagruel: *"Fais ce que tu veux!", that is, "Do as you like!", which radiates so strongly from your own books.*

You may be right. I know some sections by heart, and that Renaissance 'Bible' of François Rabelais is my second university. My *Magna Carta*... So up to the age of about twenty I would really read pretty well just for amusement, and always in bed with my cats. I used to go to bed early; it hadn't even started to go dark and I would already be in bed, reading, and the cats would be lying next to me, and I read the same things over and over again and they never failed to excite me. That's where the roots are. After twenty I began to appreciate just what books are, and what education is. Until I was twenty I was actually spiritually dead. I was always somewhere else. Even at school.

What subjects did you fail?

Czech, always. It's taken me until now to grasp what the pluperfect is.

And what school was that at, primary or secondary?

In Brno and Nymburk;[4] I was sort of thick. *Ignorantia.*

---

[4] Nymburk is a small country town about 30 miles east of Prague and the location of the brewery where Hrabal grew up (his father was the manager) and to which he constantly refers. In more recent times, the beers produced here were given names derived from the town's Hrabal 'heritage': generically

What do you think is the value of reading in adulthood, adolescence and childhood?

I would say that reading is part of how personality is formed. A child, the little child that still hasn't learned to read properly, gradually gains an overview through reading; it's a process of accretion, of getting to know the world about us. Gradually teaching you about the things that are there in school and in the wider world. The boys at school who were any good were always keen readers.

And what about those teenage years, when you were incapable of studying?

Of course, I did have that failing at secondary school of being incapable of studying. I couldn't even look at a textbook, it would send me into convulsions.

Why?

I don't know. The thing is, my book was everything outside.

Were you a bright lad?

Far from it; I was more the stupid kind, in my own way. One day, when I was in the fourth grade at primary school, some big girls from the fourth grade of the council secondary school came to fetch me and

Postřižinské pivo (after *Postřižiny* 'Cutting it short', the semi-autobiographical story set around Hrabal's early life at the brewery, on which he will have much to say later in this book), Pepinova desítka (after Uncle Pepin), Francinův ležák (after Hrabal's father), and Zlatovar (after the colour of his mother's hair). Perhaps regrettably, the own-brand Nymburk beer marketed in the 1990s by the Sainsbury chain of supermarkets, was sold under the bland and anonymous label of 'Sainsbury's Czech pilsener'.

took me to their school. The girls there weren't quite clear about Saul and his conversion to Paul. I arrived and reeled it all off pat. Afterwards Dean Nikl said: 'Girls, you ought to be ashamed!', and then 'Bohoušek, thank you', and then they took me back. That was the first and last time I shone at school.

And on the threshold of maturity?

When I grew up, that's to say, after twenty, when I got to university, I took to books totally. And ever since, since I was twenty, I've been gathering information. And with great relish. I even became obsessed with reading the ancient philosophers, Chinese poets, and so the pluperfect has gradually become my present.

You are a writer and you read philosophy. And what about the ordinary man? Why and how does he read?

Same as me. He will make his own choice of things that suit his mentality, his style, what he's had in him since childhood, and that's the kind of literature he chooses. Hence in this one country that I know, Bohemia and Moravia, reading is a matter of course. Here, when any book that has some value appears, it sells out immediately. You get queues on a Thursday and you know at once that they've must have got some bestseller or something of the kind that interests Czech readers. And it doesn't matter if they're workers or students or intellectuals; because I live in a country where people have known how to read and write for dozens of generations. Which now means that everyone wants to be a brain-surgeon and no one fancies shovelling dirt...

And where does this thirst for books come from?

I don't know. In this country there is a kind of need to read, not the way it is perhaps in some other countries. Once, long ago, Cardinal Piccolomini sent a report to Rome including the comment that in this country, that's to say in Prague, he had found old women, ordinary women, who understood Holy Scripture better than the cardinals in Rome. If you're ever on a tram in Prague you'll see that every third person is asleep and every fourth is reading. Not just newspapers, but books as well. And people are so passionately engrossed in their books that you can't miss it. Where the thirst comes from I've no idea. I don't know where this nation gets it from, though I recognize that other nations read as well. The first thing that strikes foreigners arriving here is that the man in the street is much better informed than they expected. That ordinary folk will have their little bookcase at home, and know what's in it, and they'll have a broad idea of the ins and outs of various problems in Europe or the wider world. Czechs are much better informed, and in greater depth, than, say, Germans; your Czech is somehow possessed by a yearning to know. Which also explains the mess we're in...

It strikes me that the situation in Budapest, Vienna or Warsaw is the same: every third person in the tram's asleep, and every fourth one's reading.

Yes, yes, I suspect it's because we all belong to some common awareness, as we might call it; this is that *Mitteleuropa* of which several nations have been the vehicle, including the Jews. The big cities – Budapest,

Vienna, Prague, Brno, Cracow – the Jewish thread runs through them all. The Jews had their own newspapers, and the nation with which they were living tried to catch up with them. In the Austria of last century little boys could recite the Talmud by the time they were six. And mind this: wherever a number of linguistic awarenesses intersect you will find culture. Your average citizen of Brno or Prague simply can't fail to be well-read.

Am I to understand you to be saying that there was always a greater hunger for culture in Central Europe than anywhere else?

But of course. It comes from the geography. Central Europe – the very term tells you we have no sea. And then: it was around the sea, by which I obviously mean the Mediterranean, that world culture was created. Some parts of that world culture, the Greeks, the Romans, may have got as far as Slovakia, but that's all they did – got there. So Central Europe had to create everything itself. The process of its realization, the creation of its culture, is about a thousand years old. So hereabouts, where we have no sea, we don't have that grand sense of what there is to be felt from looking out to sea. Each and every Central European wants to see the sea, and when he sees it he is struck to the well-spring of his being. Thus to compensate for having no ocean, we've had to have oceans of knowledge. We have always had to be number one: even in Christianity, even during the Reformation, even in the Baroque. In this country, at least where I come from, Bohemia – though I believe it applies right across Central Europe – information coming from the West always reached such a peak that we would take things almost *ad absurd-um*. Whether it was the Gothic, or the Baroque, we always took things to absurd lengths. And here, in Central Europe, anything that was a matter of course anywhere else became a huge event. Two trivial details: when a women first drove a car in Paris, you had a woman driving a car; but when a woman first drove a car in Prague, forty thousand people came to watch. In short, a great event; like when Josephine Baker or Mastroianni or Gérard Philipe came, they were always great events here, and still are. Not only do all these things get into the papers, but everybody wants to get involved as well. When Barbra Streisand turned up incognito, people still recognized her in the street. And they recognize writers, sportsmen, and it's an event, like what we said about whenever a good book is published, or when famous sportsmen or writers appear...

That brings us back to reading. When I was at primary school, a school where the language of instruction was Hungarian, I remember how much I enjoyed reading The Grandmother.[5]

When I first read *Babička*, also at school, it felt as if I was reading the paper. I mean, it was only much later that I found that if there's one thing written in the spirit of an age it is newspapers. Němcová was a con-

---

[5] *Babička* (1855), the best-known and universally read Czech classic by Božena Němcová (1820–62). Compulsory reading in Czechoslovak schools (hence the Slovak-Hungarian Szigeti's exposure to it) and still compulsory reading for most Czech schoolchildren, it first appeared in 1855. Though not widely known in the Anglo-Saxon world, it has been translated twice into English: as *The Grandmother: a Story of Country Life in Bohemia*, trans. Frances Gregor, Chicago, 1891; and *Granny: Scenes from Country Life*, trans. Edith Pargeter, Prague c. 1962 and Westport, Conn., 1976.

temporary of George Sand,[6] who is arty, starchy, recherché. But Němcová's is honest-to-goodness realistic, noble art. And she begins so musically: *Babička* has a preamble, almost a short poem. 'It has been a long, long time since I last gazed into that meek face... Grandmother had two sons and two daughters.' Fullstop. And off it goes. And the story unfolds as if narrated by a Chekhov or one of the American Realists; Němcová was actually ahead of her time. When we read her love-letters it was an eye-opener; she is absolutely frank in them. She also had an aptitude for collecting fairy-tales, like the Czech poet and folklorist Karel Jaromír Erben,[7] who collected the kind of fairy-tales that seemed to have disappeared; and those fairy-tales are all so hurtful. While I once read *Babička* like a newspaper, it later dawned on me that Němcová was writing for the future. It is already a fully-fledged Realism, an even severe, almost laconic Realism. A testimony. Even a kind of need to heal herself by writing. She had to write *Babička* the minute she remembered her grandmother. To write it she must have been thoroughly wretched. She wrote in order to cure herself of profound melancholia and hopelessness. And yet she managed to produce a work of optimism. And that's also the value of literature, you know; it must heal, it's no easy matter, writing, just writing – it

[6] The French woman writer George Sand (real name Aurore Dupin, 1804–76) influenced many Czech writers, including Němcová and, for example, Amálie Vrbová, who wrote under the name Jiří (that is, also 'George') Sumín (1863–1936).

[7] Karel Jaromír Erben (1811–70), known to all Czechs for his verse collection *Kytice* (A Bouquet, 1853); more compulsory reading for Czech children. An English translation by Susan Halstead, long overdue, is forthcoming.

has to have deep roots. And there are plenty of writers who write almost exclusively to keep themselves from committing suicide, or so as not to feel wretched, at rock-bottom. And morally Němcová was also shattered, yet society wanted her to put on a show and represent the new 'revived' society. Her mission and destiny, as we have said, were not comic, but tragic. Tragic! She was a noble woman with ingrained tragedy; a beauty who had to do things she would never have done had she not been forced to do them by lack of money, by having hit rock-bottom. And the Grandmother figure came to her as her salvation, even in that crude – we might say – unrefined form. She writes like a man, does Božena Němcová. It's a personal statement, but at the same time literature. And fate. And the fascination of lovers.

And what about Jan Neruda?[8]

Now you're talking. Neruda. If, as a matter of principle, I wanted to flatter him a bit, then I think my best short-stories could be, that is I'd like them to be, equal to his *Tales from the Little Quarter*,[9] which to me are the peak of perfection. There Neruda blithely juxtaposes opposites: you have him dancing with this beautiful girl, then up she gets and goes home, where her mother is lying dead. You know, it's sort of – how

[8] Jan Neruda (1834–91). The main Czech nineteenth-century prose classic, also important for several collections of verse.

[9] *Povídky malostranské* (1878), Neruda's best-known collection of stories, set in the Little Quarter (Malá strana) of Prague. In English as *Tales of Little Quarter*, trans. Edith Pargeter (Melbourne, 1957, and Westport, Conn., 1976). Like Němcová's *Babička* and Erben's *Kytice*, compulsory reading in Czech schools.

might we put it? – he's a precursor of Chekhov. And he's my teacher...

Teacher?

Of course. And he came before that whole Chekhov period.

But while your narrative is full of irony, there's no irony in Neruda. I would be more inclined to see you as continuator of the irony of Jaroslav Hašek.[10]

If you will. Neruda was a far more honourable man. He had the notion that it was addressed to someone. He was a writer with a big W. People look to him, he's a spokesman. Whereas I probably fit in the category, or rather I've adopted the mantle, of Jaroslav Hašek, who may have written for the newspapers, but his irony was of such vast dimensions that I still can't see where it ends. As for Schweik, that's something so monstrous that I'll probably not get it sussed until half an hour before I die. Old Hašek sure knew how to cover his tracks! Because don't forget that he wrote several hundred articles for the papers, articles where the irony is of such grand proportions that it all becomes a bit of a hoax. News items about broken legs, accidents, drunkards – it was Hašek who brought these to the papers. Radko Pytlík[11] has collected them all

[10] Jaroslav Hašek (1883–1923), author of *The Adventures of the Good Soldier Schweik*, three times translated into English. He wrote many other stories that are largely unfamiliar to the English reader, but see the collection *The Bachura Scandal and other Stories and Sketches*, trans. Alan Menhennet (London, 1991); it is this type of story that so impresses Hrabal.

[11] Radko Pytlík (b.1928), contemporary Czech literary critic and historian; writes chiefly on Hašek, but also on Kafka and Hrabal, whom he lists in the

and published them, and you're surprised to find that Hašek the journalist was already getting ready for what Schweik would say. He had a perfectly clear idea. The irony that came after was a matter of course; he had it ready-made and absorbed within him as a journalist. He would end an article with a complete about-turn, like a fairy-tale; that's where you find his Prague irony. In other words, he would skew a news item in such a way as to make it a bit of a hoax; the basic facts, the points of reference, are all right, yet the twist at the end raises a smile, in other words you find yourself going against the flow of information laid out in just five lines. An article might have eight lines, but the last three stand it on its head. A pirouette on a postage stamp.

Might it be said that he turned information into literature?

He had to. He had to find out what things had happened and where so that he could do a short report – Radko Pytlík has published several hundred of them. And you suddenly realize that he's my kind of author; this is the reporting that gets into books, the existential flaw in the diamond.

Although you've called Neruda your teacher, I get the feeling that your real teacher is Jaroslav Hašek.

I believe I read them both in my thirties, but Neruda is only now telling me things that he hadn't said before; you know, like when you were reading Chekhov

Czech Who's Who among the people he particularly respects. His book, *The Sad King of Czech Literature: Bohumil Hrabal* (Prague, 2000), is among the more recent titles about Hrabal available in English.

and when you read Babel's[12] *Red Cavalry*[13] and when you read Hemingway and Faulkner's stories, Neruda was sidelined by them as a sort of set book. Only now is he surfacing. Only now do I begin to see the sheer capacity of Božena Němcová. Now that I'm getting on, some of Neruda's stories have suddenly started springing up from my inner recesses and blazing with a light I hadn't seen before, you know, with all the what I'd call robustness of a writer who lived in the 1870s, and it has suddenly, belatedly, dawned on me that some of his stories might have been written in the 1920s by one of the Americans, or even a Russian. By which I mean that even we did and do have something on which to lean. It's an unfinished process, one where you carry on making discoveries. At the moment I am reading Jakub Deml's *Forgotten Light*,[14] for me the very acme of twentieth-century prose. On a par with anything the rest of the world has to offer. In how it's written and what makes it great. It has also appeared in Paris, and Paris is discovering Ladislav Klíma[15] *and* Jakub Deml. It was written sometime in the Thirties and gives the impression that he wrote it in a week. It's

[12] Izaak Babel (1894–1941). A Russian follower of the school of Maupassant and Chekhov, in which the comic story is elevated to the level of irony – hence his significance to Hrabal's development

[13] Interestingly, in both Czech and English Babel's *Konarmia* (Horse Army) – the word is a Soviet neologism – is mistranslated as 'Red Cavalry'. The collection is rich in irony, but is not meant as criticism of the 1917 October Revolution itself or of the Polish campaign which is the background for the stories.

[14] *Zapomenuté světlo* (1934). Jakub Deml (1878–1961), Czech Catholic priest, prose-writer, poet and critic. Described, *inter al.*, as a writer of emotionally explosive and deeply meditative works.

[15] Ladislav Klíma (1878–1928), Czech moral nihilist and philosophical Expressionist, ignored by the Communists and perhaps best-known for his aphorisms.

got focus, a script like the best Fellini film, and it's even cut like a film. Deml is a past-master at cutting.[16] So in short I'm proud to be here, from Central Europe, and that I belong here, with these literary pinnacles, as I acknowledge them. For me the pinnacles of prose are: Hašek, Kafka, Weiner,[17] Klíma, Deml; you know they too were all a little bit *maudit*, you understand? I like Karel Čapek:[18] he was a man in a dinner-jacket, and he represented society, the President, and the Pen Club, and he was a gentleman. But somehow or other it was the French taught me to love those *poètes maudits*, Villon, Baudelaire, you know, more the ones who had to fight for things, and even found asylum in gaol; they didn't have an easy time of it, which is probably what gave them their genius. Villon for one. A sort of heritage of *la douce France*, simply a bequest from those *poètes maudits*. Hašek and Klíma also knew all about them. They were *maudits* themselves...

So at university you became thoroughly addicted to books.

Yes. When I was twenty I became so addicted to books and education that I not only studied for and took a degree in law, but I also attended philosophy

[16] The significance of film technique, cutting especially, will become apparent as the interview progresses. It is a key creative device throughout Hrabal's work.

[17] Richard Weiner (1884–1937), Czech writer given to linguistic and formal experimentation, and journalist – Paris correspondent of the pro-government *Lidové noviny*.

[18] Karel Čapek (1890–1938), perhaps the best known (with Hašek) and most extensively translated Czech writer (stories, novels, plays; he also translated from French literature). A strong sympathiser with Masarykian 'humanitism' and a member of the 'Castle' circle (the Czech inter-war establishment). He is also the inventor of the word 'robot' (see his play *RUR*).

lectures; I was taken with Schopenhauer and the Greeks. I went to lectures on Surrealism, on the whole of French literature; I won't even begin to list everything I read, or all the European cities I went to, what galleries I visited, how many books on art I read. As things have turned out I can be my own source of enlightenment...

I expect that in all that learning you read the poètes maudits *before getting to, say, Neruda.*

Oh yes. I didn't get to know Neruda until much later; I began with American and French literature in translation. I couldn't fail to run up against the Surrealists, Apollinaire, and of course Baudelaire, Rimbaud. Baudelaire's sentences can be read at any time. Those dead men are more than alive...

In the Thirties you had the huge advantage of being able to read the best of the world's literature in Czech.

I should say so! It's amazing. Karel Čapek, who never wrote a poem, was one of the first to produce, in 1920, an anthology of modern French poetry, and above all he brought the main thing to our notice: Apollinaire. Baudelaire, Verlaine and Rimbaud had all been translated by the previous generation. Apollinaire was something of a *magnus parens*, simply a grand sire, both for Seifert[19] and for Vítězslav Nezval,[20] that

---

[19] Jaroslav Seifert (1901–86), perceived as one of the greatest modern Czech poets (Nobel Prize 1984).
[20] Vítězslav Nezval (1900–58), major twentieth-century Czech poet, adherent of Poetism (a uniquely Czech movement in poetry, typified by imaginative free association) and Surrealism, which also comes out in his prose, such as *Valérie a týden divů* (in English as *Valerie and her Week of Wonders* [Prague, 2005]).

is, for the avant-garde group of Poetists centred on *Devětsil*.[21] Nezval was so bewitched by him that he almost became his devoted disciple. Poetism was an original and precious tie between the home-grown modernist tradition and the European avant-garde. It was a product of the Czech environment. And of course Apollinaire meant a lot to me too; that shows just how great he was. And then there were translations of American poetry. So it's entirely fair to say that we missed nothing in those days...

It's surely also much to the credit of the publishing houses that you missed nothing.

That was typical. In those days you didn't have public educationists.[22] That's more recent. Those people were society's enlighteners; they felt it their duty to ensure that the nation was as well informed as possible. Our small-nation politics was culture. And so we had our *Kulturträger* in them, the publishers – Štorch-Marien,[23] or Melantrich;[24] even small towns

A time- server in his later life, with his ode to Stalin and other 'red' poems.
[21] *Devětsil* (Butterbur), a group of Czech socialist poets, critics, dramatists, architects etc. active in the 1920s. The move of some away from 'proletarian', collectivist art around 1924 gave rise to Poetism. The choice of the movement's name is associated with the literal meaning of the plant's name in Czech: 'nine powers', i.e. in alternative medicine it is a plant with many restorative properties – as anti-convulsive, anti-febrile, anthelminthic, diuretic, laxative, in the treatment of wounds that are slow to heal and for the relief of haemorrhoids.
[22] The Czech word here, *osvětáři*, implies people involved in such activities as the Workers' Educational Association in Britain or other broadly improving campaigns.
[23] Otakar Štorch-Marien (1897–1974), Czech publisher, cultural historian and memoirist, founder of the Aventinum publishing-house, whose name survived, despite nationalization.
[24] This respected and still extant publishing house owes its name to Jiří

had their little publishing houses for whom it was a matter of honour to publish the odd best-seller. In the new age, under socialism, these private publishers disappeared of course, but publishing remained, and so now we have Mladá fronta,[25] Československý spisovatel[26] or Odeon.[27] And those who decide what's to be published do try to ensure that works of value appear, works that contribute to education and knowledge. And for the writer that is both a good and a bad thing...

I'd like you to say a word on how today's publishers keep abreast of contemporary literature elsewhere in the world.

Things could be better. I miss many of the poets we only know from magazines, in snippets. But we do have publishing houses like Odeon; their last book to captivate me was William Styron's *Sophie's Choice.* An outstanding author, outstanding translation, but again you can't get hold of it. And there you have it – just like in Budapest: as soon as a decent book appears, it's sold out the same day. So in a nutshell, things could be better. I would say that these days books aren't published by supply and demand, but that publishing, well, it's cultural politics. If you take a good look at what's on offer, you don't even want to know. Then of

Melantrich z Aventina (1511–80), one of the best-known and most ambitious Czech sixteenth-century printers and publishers.

[25] The publishing house of the socialist youth organization; it also published a popular daily newspaper under the same name (= Young Front). The company still exists, as does the newspaper, now published as *MFDnes.*

[26] That is, 'Czechoslovak Writer' – the publishing house of the Union of Czechoslovak Writers. Superseded since 1989 by Český spisovatel.

[27] Publishers of 'quality' and 'coffee-table' books.

course a lot depends on whether there is enough paper or not. But what can you do about it?

Do you, as a writer, have an image of your reader? Do you think about him as you write?

Definitely not. That's quite out of the question because – if I may talk about it now, when I'm still only seventy, and yet it's only now beginning to dawn – the more I look back on how I first started writing verse,[28] the better I see that I've always written for myself. It's because I'm really so intoxicated by the environment in which and through which I move, and I only go home to sleep; ever since childhood I've been among people and I don't even realize that when I speak about myself, about the landscape of my affairs, I'm afraid that I'm also talking about others. Thanks to expressing myself in extremely subjective terms and being my own first reader, I can actually sense that I'm writing for myself; and only later do I discover that those other people have been stealing my words, that I've actually been speaking on their behalf. So my extremely subjective discourse is suddenly objective. Obviously it's like a pair of bellows, that's to say I take a deep breath then breathe out again. I simply breathe in a certain amount of information, and as I write I'm exhaling it. I use a typewriter, and I can write so very fast that sometimes the typewriter reaches a throughput of one page in eight minutes; so I get all charged

[28] Hrabal's verse is the least well known part of his work. For a recent appraisal in English see David Chirico: 'Towards a typology of Hrabal's intertextuality: Bohumil Hrabal and Giuseppe Ungaretti', in David Short (ed.): *Bohumil Hrabal (1914-97). Papers from a Symposium* (London, 2004), pp. 11-33.

up, like an accumulator. I'm not a spokesman for all readers, just for one category; every writer has his own sort of reader with whom he shares ideas as to what the world should be like and how one should behave in society and what he may demand of society, and what is fun for him and what is bad luck. And in that sense I have precisely those several hundred thousand readers with whom, you might say, I share a common denominator. They keep you on your toes and it's ... a damn' tricky business ...

So you do think about your readers. On your own admission you write for readers who share your ideas.

Because those people of mine speak the same language. I operate in the environment of Prague irony, of things which are deliberately a bit different in meaning. Those people only find things out by talking and living; they don't know everything at once, *a priori*, but only *ex post*. It's only after they've known disappointment, or been over-enthusiastic, or found themselves in a situation they didn't expect to be in, that they, in it and through it, discover the fact, and it is precisely that which has, as we might put it, an ironic and, at the same time, dramatic charge. And since I collect that current of irony from simple people, there is some truth in the suggestion that I write about them and for them. I'm forever in amongst them, so I keep picking up juice and once I'm fully charged, I quickly sit down at the typewriter.

So these are the roots of your writing so fast and with such tremendous energy?

I suspect those roots have social aspects. You see, all my glorious jobs have lasted four years: four years at Kladno iron and steel works, four years at the S. K. Neumann Theatre, four years in a paper recycling plant, and four years on the railways, and when I was at Kladno, I didn't have much time, and yet I did. Do you know why? Because in those days two or three hours were enough and I would get writing. I used to write in a sort of dense haze; I would get a sudden urge to write, and if the urge coincided with my time off, I would write and write and write. Otherwise I would mope and languish about the workplace, the haze would descend and I didn't have the time to fashion it into words. Three hours those days was a whacking great time, a bushel of time. Which is also why I learned to type so fast; I've already told you, my typewriter would achieve a rate of a page in eight minutes. Then, for those four years when I worked at Kladno, every second week I was on the afternoon shift. That was the gift to end all gifts; I would write all morning, it was a huge treat; I was the king of time. Nowadays I console myself with what Hrubín[29] used to say: 'I say, Bohouš, are you in the same bad way as me? Whenever I have to fill in a postal-cheque form and take it to the post-office, not just that day is completely buggered, but the next one as well. Do you find the same?' I used to reply: 'Not yet, František, not yet. But is it really that bad?' – And these days I know

<hr>

[29] František Hrubín (1910–71), Czech writer and dramatist and the most important twentieth-century author of verse for children.

that I am in just the same bad way as František then. And I copied out that plaint of Oskar Kokoschka, that when I was young, Sunday lasted a whole month; today a year doesn't even amount to a week for me. Ah yes, when I was young I didn't write, I just read; I would read *Master Naughty*; I knew it by heart, and I used to crease up laughing like Uncle Pepin,[30] and read it again and again. And look around me.

Which brings us to Uncle Pepin, to the family story-telling, the stories told you by your mother, Uncle Pepin, the workmen at the brewery and the good people of Nymburk.

I always had a kind of complex about my mother. The boys I knocked around with, they had mothers who looked like mothers; they wore aprons and were all messy from house-work, just ordinary women. Whereas my mother was more like an older sister. Forever laughing, forever putting on a show, and I was sorry she wasn't like the mothers of the others. – Oh yes, things were different at our house. When I was ten, Uncle Pepin came to see us. He lived and ate with us, working in the brewery, so the whole household was like a merry-go-round, and the central pillar it turned around, that was Uncle Pepin. And we would ask him questions that were sometimes quite ridiculous, so all I remember from childhood is Uncle Pepin and the stories he told us, and how we would provoke him into talking. Our brewery was alive with Uncle Pepin's shouting, our laughter, the chaotic conversations, such

---

[30] Hrabal's crazy Uncle Pepin was a major formative element in Hrabal's domestic background. He appears in his own right in several of Hrabal's semi-autobiographical works.

crazy conversations, rather dadaist in their way, but not like the Dadaism of Zurich – just about erecting the absurdity of talk against the absurdity of war and the world – but Dadaism of the Prague kind. Prague Dadaism is the term used by Teige[31] or Vítězslav Nezval, in other words the Poetists. Teige even wrote a study on it in *A world that smells nice*,[32] that was sometime round 1930, and I think Prague Dadaism figured in the theatre as well. More pirouettes on a postage stamp.

Are you thinking of early 1927, when the Liberated Theatre split and one part, with Jiří Frejka[33] and E. F. Burian,[34] set up the Dada theatre, otherwise known as U Nováků (the present ABC Theatre), where, under the name 'Liberated Theatre', after 1931, Voskovec and Werich[35] evolved their conception of the theatre as Dadaist and lyricized farce? Or do you mean Burian's 'D', which sprang up at the end of 1933?

I mean everyone who played Prague Dada.

[31] Karel Teige (1900–51), Czech critic and art theorist, a major exponent, spokesman and/or co-founder of the major inter-war movements of Proletarian Art (1920), Poetism (1924) and Czech Surrealism (1934).

[32] *Svět, který voní* (1930).

[33] Jiří Frejka (1904–52), theatre director and theorist, a leader of the Czech Avant-garde; co-founder of the Liberated Theatre (1925) in Prague and founder of his own Dada Theatre (1927); member of the National Theatre (1930–45), Director (1945–50) of the Vinohrady Theatre, another of Prague's main houses.

[34] E[mil] F[rantišek] Burian (1904–59), theatre director, playwright, writer and composer; a leader of the Czech Avant-garde; Founded D 34 theatre in 1933.

[35] Jiří Voskovec (1905–81) and Jan Werich (1905–80) collaborated in avant-garde theatre and film for many years, both in inter-war and immediate post-war Prague and, during the war, in New York. In 1948 Voskovec emigrated, first to Paris then (1950) to the USA. After the war, Werich remained in Prague until his death, as actor, songwriter and raconteur. The Liberated Theatre and US periods of their career are further remembered for their collaboration with the musician Jaroslav Ježek (1906–42), who also collaborated on their films.

And had intellectual ambitions?

I would call it something like Prague irony. Their mainspring was Charlie Chaplin, but they also followed in the tradition of American cinema slapstick, and the old Italian *commedia dell'arte*. Chaplin's early slapstick films are also dadaist. And yet so terribly lyrical...

And Uncle Pepin too?

Pepin absolutely. Pepin was literally a character like Charlie Chaplin, or Lupino Lane, or Frigo;[36] Frigo was melancholic and intellectual. Uncle Pepin was just the same as Chaplin.

And Uncle Pepin never stopped telling stories.

Right, but he could also act, and he could dance. Uncle Pepin danced exquisitely, but the way madmen dance, more like how they dance today; he danced to the beat of the music even in those days. And he was a kind of linguistic catalyst, because he had such an amazing way of expressing his ideas and spicing his humour with moral precepts. He was my Muse, disguised as a cobbler and maltster.

And your mother? Did she also tell you stories and spin you yarns?

In her own special way she did – through the theatre, the household and society. She was extremely good as a housewife, and yet she had this peculiar awareness; she was a born bohemian and enjoyed play-acting, in fact she was in theatre all her life. I remember

[36] The reference here is to *Frigo na mašině*, as Buster Keaton's film *The General* is known in Czech.

how she would go to rehearsals and first nights. And she kept house. Even in that little town there was an enthusiastic theatre group, and my mother – and people coming from Prague said this too, and visiting actors – was much liked. She was devoted to the theatre, she had considerable talent, and that talent for theatre was borne along with the same kind of bohemianism. As much as she was a bohemian, she knew how to laugh, she loved company and always had to be the centre of attention. If ever there was a dance on, my mother and her partners were the best dancers. Of an evening, in that little town, she was always strikingly prettily dressed as well; she was gorgeous and we lads would read her body language, since in that way too she would talk about herself and the world. Her story-telling ran through the household, the theatre and society.

How many of you were there in the family?

I have a brother, he lives next-door to me in Kersko.[37] We've never had a row and I visit him every weekend; and I still haven't had a bust-up with my sister-in-law either, which is a major achievement. But my brother has such a command of irony that he should have been a writer...

You have spoken about books, the roots you discovered in childhood, but I assume those roots also include your mother's play-acting.

Oh no, no. I was none too keen on my mother's acting, I think I was really a bit embarrassed for her.

---

[37] Kersko, actually Kerské Woods, near Lysá nad Labem and about 15 miles NE of Prague, was Hrabal's second home for much of his professional life.

I didn't like it when she laughed, or was affected, or tried to be the centre of attention. I had a sort of complex, of course not of the Oedipus kind, but simply arising from my mother's being the centre of attention. It left me rather sullen, and my father, Francin, he was often sullen too, having to put up with it. You could hardly call him happy about it. He was glad when it was time to go home from a dance or party. He preferred home. On the other hand, mother did do everything that was needed about the house. She kept two goats and some pigs, she would clean and tidy, sometimes with the maids, but mostly on her own, and then she'd be off. She'd put on a nice suit and march off to a rehearsal at the theatre; that, I would say, was the sort of high point for her. She liked to show off, she liked talking, she liked acting and she liked going on about the theatre. She would read about it, all the reviews, and she had to go and see everything that was on in Prague. And so people would come to the house; mother had several friends she acted with. They were hugely interested and informed not only about their own current play, but about plays generally, in short just like people at the big city theatres. I had my ideals, my literary ideals, you know, Franz Kafka and the others, while she had, say, Andula Sedláčková,[38] on whom she would model herself, doing her hair like Andula's and adopting her gestures.

[38] Anna (familiarly Andula) Sedláčková (1887–1967), popular actress and member of the National Theatre company 1905–38 (with breaks). She ran her own Anna Sedláčková Theatre during the war (1939–44).

During your childhood at home Uncle Pepin acted as a kind of linguistic catalyst; he was suited to the kind of excitability that thrills the senses and the imagination.

Not half! His delivery was unbelievable!

If we think about it, he was actually presenting you with fairy-tales. Doesn't that inspire you to write books for children?

I was once commissioned to write a fairy-tale for children. It was called *Ox-Eye Daisy*[39] and was published by Mladá fronta in 1962. It's the only thing I've ever written for children, an exception in effect. I did include it in one later collection, sort of to show I knew children existed, but apart from that it's never entered my head to write for children. Because my head is always already full of the book I need to be getting on with, you see. I have the text in front of me, hanging in the air, and I am all charged up with the disquiet that looks for, and then finds, the common denominator, and I have to write it down. Right now, if someone came along to commission a play or a children's book, I just wouldn't talk to him; I've never had any regard for commissions because I always think that the book I'm supposed to be writing, like now, has to be finished and I have to take care not to die. Because I'm the only one that can write it and it's me that it's dangling in front of; and what I have already written is no longer of the slightest interest to me. So my sole concern is – and it's really something of a luxury, you see, to have as my sole concern me myself. Just my own problems, but then my problems are actually general

[39] *Kopretina*, published 1965, notwithstanding Hrabal's assertion in this sentence.

ones. I am their usher towards the common denominator. Note that: I have never described myself as a writer; I have always said I am a recorder, or minute-taker. Most of those lovely stories I hear from others. So I collect them, rather as Božena Němcová collected fairy-tales; I collect a mass of stories in my head until I've got a whole chandelier, all those crystal droplets. Then when I'm supercharged and my head is threatening to burst, I have to sit down, at the typewriter. And as you inhale, then exhale, the ordinary mechanism of breathing, so I carry on writing until all those images have drained away – the images that had been agitating me, pushing and shoving inside me like kids playing in a sandpit – and then I am empty again and things can start filling up once more.

Do you have any family?

A wife yes, no children. Which may be why I don't write children's books. If I'd had children, I expect I would have written something for them as well – perhaps. But it's also true that if I had children, where would the writing be? I'm sure I would look after the children and not even think about writing, because, for me, wife and family mean more than anything else. But if you don't have children, what should you do? You might as well go hang yourself, or write. Writing is a defence against boredom, but it's also a cure for melancholy; then it's quite nice when a book comes out. But if you haven't got children, what should you really do? Carry on writing, to cure yourself of gloom and loneliness. But because children are also prone to dive into gloom and loneliness, I would write for them after all. Yes, I would write that book, but I would write it for the big children that are inside grown-ups. Look, it's probably extremely difficult to write for children. We could say that the number one children's writer in this country is František Hrubín. And whenever I read him I am in awe of his skill. He must have been first and foremost a grown-up child, but I don't think I'm anything of the kind; I'm more the naughty child, I'm a Master Naughty. – Or, look at it this way: sometimes I take stock when money is being discussed. But money is no help; you need something inside you. But if you have a family with children, you need money for them. You see, if I did also have the gift of writing, but, say, four children with it, then this one would want a piano, that one a motor-bike, and another goodness knows what, you understand, so then I'd have to try, I would try for the children's sake. – But why should I write for children since I write for myself? I am the first. I can grant myself that luxury. That's what I was taught by Baudelaire and Rimbaud, who are way beyond my range. They wrote for themselves. Baudelaire for one was well off; in the last twenty years I've also been well off. So I can afford this luxury, I mean now I can afford to do what as a young man I only dreamed of. Write relaxed prose, just like those heroes of mine; as Rimbaud put it, stuff with a style, a spell in hell; like Dr Kafka wrote, right? He also wrote for the healing effect; it was a luxury for him too; he would write as if he were trying to treat himself. He had terrible TB, so he simply erected his texts as a cure. And something tells me that Arthur Schopenhauer was another one who wrote as if therapeutically. While I was studying law at university, Professor Fischer[40] lectured on the philosophy of Arthur Schopenhauer, but Schopenhauer had begun to interest me a year before that, because I'd begun to read Kant, and there in the foreword it said that in some senses Schopenhauer was Kant's successor. So I started going to the lectures, I went off and bought the books, and I had to learn German. Imagine that opposite the Law Faculty there used to be a bookshop – it disappeared during the bombing of Prague – and I bought five volumes there. They were Schopenhauer's *Die Welt als Wille und Vorstellung*, black-bound, with hand-notes and underlinings, and new words jotted in the margins. I could tell from the handwriting that they came from the library of Ladislav Klíma, who had been a great Schopenhauer expert. And of course Schopenhauer was just right: at the time I was living in Nymburk, I would go for endless walks, I enjoyed going swimming, and I merged with Nature. For me Nymburk was truly a beautiful town where time had stood still,[41] and Schopenhauer speaks of this in his philosophy. That art of withdrawal started with Plato and passed through Indian philosophy, unendeavouring endeavour, that *tat-twam asi!* – 'it is you!', the art of mysticism. So you see, that young man who was no good at studying actually knew all this subconsciously, from walking about the darkened brewery and through the night

---

[40] Otakar Fischer (1883–1938), Professor of German at Charles University (from 1917). A major Czech literary critic, theorist and historian, also poet, playwright and translator.

[41] The phrase alludes to Hrabal's *Městečko, kde se zastavil čas* (The Little Town Where Time Stood Still), *samizdat* 1973, then Innsbruck, 1978.

into the orchard and from gazing at the stars. The reason I couldn't learn was because as dusk gathered and the first star came out I would spill across into it and have a sense of infinite gratification. That I'd actually reached all the way up to that star. I would go up to the top of the brewery, onto the roofs, an utterly beautiful night, and I would experience that 'procreation in the Beautiful'[42] of the world of Plato. I didn't like progress, I liked things to stand still, and I read all that in Schopenhauer, that that was the real thing. '*Alle Liebe ist Mitleid*' – compassion even with animals. If ever they couldn't find me, I'd be lying in the cattle-shed, with the oxen; the oxen loved me – we had two yokes of them. Or with the horses, just casually touching each other; in other words that kind of unwanting of mine. And I'm not really in favour of my people being in any sense progressive; I am more the dreamy, perpetual adolescent who can apprehend beautiful things. Aesthetics became my ethics. Aesthetic perception. And because the brewery was on the edge of town and the Elbe so beautiful, the meadows so beautiful, and that bell-jar of the sky... – add to that the sun and bathing in the river, and the rowing-boats, I was surrounded by children; children loved me, little girls, boys, and so I had a full boatload of them. I felt like a super-dad. Can you understand? Even in the evening, when we sat about on the footbridges, I would be surrounded by children; even in Libeň

---

[42] Cf., for example, the words attributed to Diotima, 'a woman of Mantinea', during a discussion of the function of Love: 'The function is that of procreation in what is beautiful, and such procreation can be either physical or spiritual.' Plato: *The Symposium*, trans. W. Hamilton (Penguin Books, 1951, p. 86).

I had other people's children. Whenever they could they would come to the house on Na hrázi street and ask questions, or they would come along anyway, like stray cats, because they felt they belonged; coexistence without the need even for talking. I have never talked to animals no matter how much I have been as one with them. And I reckon that was all there in Schopenhauer, who carried within him the Orient, India, that Indian philosophy of endeavouring unendeavour. It's only now that I've begun to like Hegel a bit. Because I'm fifty years older now, when I run across him I suddenly find I'm in the same boat with him as when he was trying to raise model citizens. If you're a postman, you have to be in effect a transcendental postman, and if you're a coachman, then you're a transcendental coachman, and if you're a president, well you have to be one; each and every one must have his own ethics in what he does. Although I'm a lawyer, I'm no respecter of the state; the state is an organization, a pyramid, that's how it has to be, and that's supposed to make me happy? Any more than I'm an respecter of the army. But Hegel was even the creator of the Prussian state, creator of the Prussian, and so also the tsarist army; they all adopted everything from him! So I sort of didn't accept him; I was stupid, or maybe not. But I did have the impression that he was also the creator of Prussian militarism, and I don't like that. So I didn't identify with him; after all, I was twenty-five, even less, when I was ploughing through Schopenhauer, that is *Die Welt als Wille und Vorstellung*; that's where you find those swipes at Hegel. And Friedrich Nietzsche says: 'We Germans are Hegelians, whether we will or not.' And what came of that? The Germans wanting to be racially the best, causing total war and then totally losing everything.

Since this literature had such an impact on you, I assume you were also influenced by Sigmund Freud.

I was influenced by his book on hysteria; it's really a collection of essays. He was a master of style. In other words I was excited by his manner of describing his cases and his approach to the matter. But my way to Freud was via the Surrealists, who saw him as one of their precursors. *Traumdeutung*, for instance. There is a painting about the Surrealists – I don't know who did it – but Freud is there, and Dostoyevsky, looking true to life, with the group of Surrealists. That is, Freud and the way he did his examinations, with that stream of subconsciousness, is identified with the automatic texts of such Surrealists as André Breton, Philippe Soupault[43] and Artaud,[44] and Crevel...[45] It might be said that Freud's psychoanalysis gave them a method, that disturbed people are not reprehensible, but remarkable... that Freud's method helps one get at the essence of man... His clients were all disturbed, but how they expressed themselves was almost poetic. And the Surrealists' predilection for the deranged was as

[43] Philippe Soupault (1897–1977), co-author, with André Breton, of what is agreed to be the first Surrealist work, *Magnetic Fields* (1920).
[44] Antonin Artaud (1896–1948), French director, actor and poet, member of the Surrealist movement and forerunner of the Theatre of the Absurd. His studies on the 'Theatre of Cruelty' inspired generations of theatre practitioners from the 1950s.
[45] André Crevel (1900–35 [suicide]), one of the leading French Surrealist poets; a writer of despair and revolt.

great as my own. That includes my uncle, his way of telling stories and really his whole life; through all his shouting and story-telling he was really treating himself. In other words, the stories he told us at home, the yarns he spun to girls in the pubs, it was all a kind of therapy, as if he was one of Herr Freud's patients. And this spontaneity of ours – my relation to him is also *a priori* spontaneous, well, I am so much one with my uncle that I have even adopted his style, his stream of narrative, and when I take up the scissors, I cut it all up and recompose it into my own whole, and so it's literature. But the beginning is always a great stream of subconsciousness, but that's what my uncle always taught me and that's how I do things to this day. I am fascinated by one particular book of Freud's. And it's quite a small one. Take *Zur Psychopathologie des Alltagslebens*. What are my stories? Psycho-pathology of the contemporary everyday. What are Schweik's stories? They're psycho-pathology of the everyday. In Freud it's supported by scientific argument. But there is one little book, a small tome that came out at the very turn of the century – something tells me it was actually in 1900 – *The Future of an Illusion*. And it's all about the future of the illusion of whether human society can exist without its kings, presidents and archbishops. And as he alleges, it may one day be possible, but we all have to be sons. The minute we have a father, from that moment and by that father a kind of obedience is created, and the beginnings of that pyramid we find in Hegel; in other words it is the future of an illusion – that of living without fathers... And then I'm also fascinated by Freud because he finished writing what

Josef Breuer had begun.[46] He was the one who actually hit on psychoanalysis and wrote it down, but he abandoned it in time, because he was a Christian. Because he had begun to enter the chamber which a Christian should not enter. Whereas I believe Freud entered it with no sense of guilt.

What chamber is that?

The sphere of the erotic and sexual, that area of seeking what's forbidden. Because Christian faith is the awareness that, given the way we are, the way we live, our very genes have become set by that thousand-year culture; we're aware we can enter, but we have a sense of guilt. Whereas he, as a Jew, could still enter without sensing shame or guilt. And he completed the job – Freud, not Breuer; Breuer was the first to codify it, but I think he gave it up in 1882. You know, hypnotizing people... Female patients always fell in love with him, as they did with Freud. So Breuer would cure one at the cost that she, this young woman, fell in love with him; but he had a wife. But he knew where he was actually heading; through science he had reached zones never before seen and previously undreamed-of, and so he immediately took his wife off on a honeymoon trip to Venice and wanted no more to do with it. That was in the period 1882-83-84. But Freud in this country? I don't know what writer would build on him, though maybe, in a literary manner, Vítězslav Nezval did in his *Chain of Fortune*,[47] but there he was

[46] Josef Breuer (1842–1925) collaborated with Freud 1882–95; his own 'cathartic method' anticipates Freud's 'analytical method'.
[47] The novel *Řetěz štěstí* (1936), in which Nezval, reminiscent here of Breton,

operating with the Freud concept because the Surrealists were there. And wherever there were Surrealists there was the subconscious, praised as primal. And the subconscious is another of those foundations, I mean the playfulness, and it's also in *A world that smells nice*, by the æsthetician of Poetism, Karel Teige.[48] Fascination with play.

And where does Ladislav Klíma fit in here? What do you find remarkable about Klíma?

The Hungarian or Polish reader would certainly find his earliest works remarkable – in both literary and philosophical terms. I mean the philosophical writings *A Second and Eternity*,[49] and then a whole series of letters where he starts from Nietzsche and his philosophy and transforms it in terms of ludibrionism. He also wrote literature, in the book *Glorious Nemesis*,[50] which appeared during the First [Czechoslovak] Republic, as did his novel *The Sufferings of Prince Sternenhoch*.[51]

elevates spontaneity and subconscious processes to the guiding principle of creativity in art.

[48] See Note 31, 32.

[49] The collection of essays, *Vteřina a věčnost* (1927). As the editors of the Collected Works edition point out, Hrabal is wrong in including it among Klíma's 'early works', since it was actually the *last* text published in Klíma's lifetime; his true first work, *Svět jako vědomí a nic* (The world as awareness and the néant, 1904) was, however, also philosophical. (See *Sebrané spisy Bohumila Hrabala*, Vol. 17, p. 380.)

[50] The novella *Slavná Nemesis* (1932), in which Klíma describes, in a love story set against the backdrop of the Alps, the yearning for true, absolute knowledge.

[51] *Utrpení knížete Sternenhocha* (1928), described by Klíma himself as a 'grotesque romaneetto', is a fictitious record of the marriage of a degenerate German aristocrat and expresses the urge to escape from the strictures of physicality.

And under the present republic a selection of his works has appeared as *Seconds of Eternity*, compiled by Josef Zumr,[52] and that's also quite substantial. Now, under socialism, certain texts have appeared that the previous 'bourgeois' republic refused to print; no one had wanted to carry the can for the depths he plumbs, the depths of the erotic, the depths of obscenity, and yet he always counterbalanced it with a tremendous charge of philosophy... Some years ago his *Sufferings of Prince Sternenhoch* appeared in West Germany with illustrations by Jiří Kolář,[53] and now a Klíma selection has appeared in Paris, 'like a time-bomb', as the critics have put it hyperbolically, and so Paris is beginning to discover Central Europe.

But what does Klíma mean to you?

Well, for me he sort of goes without saying. He was a gigantic figure. The same kind of figure as Hašek.

I don't understand...

He was simply a chap who had an unimaginable adventure; his whole life was a gigantic adventure, a drunkard who was prosperous, but who, like Baudelaire, had squandered everything by the time he was twenty; in his youth he simply blew the lot. Klíma...

---

[52] *Vteřiny věčnosti* (1967). Josef Zumr (b. 1928), influential Czech philosopher and historian of philosophy, æsthetician, and contributing editor of Hrabal's works (and co-editor of the new edition of the works of T. G. Masaryk). In the 1950s he and his wife Jiřina were part of the Hrabal circle in Libeň.

[53] Jiří Kolář (1914–2002), Czech poet, translator, essayist and graphic artist. Lived in France from 1978.

I still don't understand. After all, the Hungarians know Hašek, but not Klíma.

Well, that is interesting, that really is interesting. I mean, Hašek is a proletarian, his mode of expression, his expressive realism is extremely communicative, while you need to read your way into Klíma; the key to Klíma is always a minimally exact symbol, and his style is always more like high literature. Mind you, sometimes very, very wounding. Klíma is my champion, my number one...

How do you mean, 'wounding'?

Well, in simple terms, he writes about the things we describe as obscene, and we know they are. He is the king of obscenity, or the king of piss-taking. He could never publish his *White Sow*,[54] not even during the First Republic, because it's really a life of Christ, where the characters are Christ and the twelve apostles and Christ is the leader of a band of robbers and highwaymen who are his friends. And the white sow is more or less the Virgin Mary, so it all takes place in a Christian world. Except that when Klíma takes the mickey he goes the whole hog, but he was always writing more for himself. And writing for himself and his friends, that's what made him *maudit*; he is that *poète maudit* who frittered his life away on writing and alcohol. For him, writing was self-realization; there are whole bundles, whole heaps of pages that haven't been published. Not perhaps because they're unpublishable, but be-

---

[54] *Bílá svině*, an 'episode' for a 'grand novel', published only posthumously in *Vteřiny věčnosti* (Note 52) and then in the critical edition of the *Velký román* (Grand Novel, 1996), of which the French edition appeared in 1991.

cause there's no publisher to finance it; it's all so utterly ludibrionistic and solipsistic, he keeps stressing 'I am god', in other words he can get away with a lot, though not everything, see? He wasn't a member of any group. He was a sharply defined man who lived in Prague at the Hotel Krása and who was always smoking a cigar or a pipe. When smoking was banned in Prague trams, he took to walking. And he was always travelling about the Bohemian countryside: there is one story, about sixty pages of text, where, having arrived in Cholupice from Zbraslav, he's sitting in the pub writing down what he'd been thinking about, what his sub-conscious had been serving up, every beautiful or obscene image, and what he could hear, but above all see, in the pub; he kept jotting it all down. He would order another beer, or a *viertel* of rum; he was a great bohemian and in his ludibrionism he was genuinely childlike. An artless child sitting on the threshold of a gin-palace.

When we were talking about reading, I forgot one question: is there a book or books that you re-read every year?

You've remembered that at just the right moment, since Klíma's letters are one thing I do read every year. Then I also re-read *Cinnamon Shops* by the Polish author Bruno Schulz,[55] and Lao Tzu's *Canonical Book of Vir-*

---

[55] Bruno Schulz (1892–1942), Polish writer, translator and painter; influenced by Expressionism. *Cinnamon Shops* (*Sklepy cynamonowe*, 1933 [dated 1934]) is a collection of 15 short stories set in a pre-war Jewish *shtetl*. It has been published in English (London, 1963; trans. Celina Wieniawska); a later edition, with the stories re-arranged, is under the title *Street of Crocodiles* in a combined collection, *The Fictions of Bruno Schulz* (London, 1988). A dramatization was performed as *Street of Crocodiles* at the Old Vic in the early 1990s.

tues.[56] That's my annual Rite of Spring, including the thunder of April...

And are they, that is Ladislav Klíma, Lao Tzu and those ordinary everyday heroes, a point of departure for you?

It's more that ludibrionism thing. In Ladislav Klíma that's everything; he is an outstanding philosopher and even saw himself as a successor to Nietzsche, stressing precisely that playful aspect, but play in the metaphysical sense. It's almost like a god playing, playing for everything, going for broke, like when you're playing *Färbel* and stake your all, your whole existence, when you want to discover what you are and what the others are. So if I were to borrow something from Freud, it would be his method, the psychoanalytical text that comes very close to the Catholic aural confession, while my confession is in writing. In other words, it was really only when I got down to writing that I began to discover what my actual essence was. It's been my task from adolescence right down to today: only when the text is written down do I learn, or discover *a posteriori* from it, all the things I've revealed about myself. This is the material I work with afterwards. As I said, by the method of cutting they use to make a film;[57] I cut it up and cut bits out and put it together. I think it's a bit like good journalism, where the journalist doesn't write down everything, but only the things that strike him as central.

[56] That is, the *Tao-te Qing*, the primary Taoist text.
[57] See Note 16.

You say that through writing you learn what your own essence is. And what have you learned so far?

Now I can look back on myself, as a seventy-year-old gentleman, I find I've gone in a sort of sinusoid. I've got this little idea about myself that I began with totally reflexive lyricism, you might say impressionism; always on the look-out for embellishments, metaphors; but over these forty years it has happened so often that I've suddenly got to the bottom of my pre-ordained essence and have kept having these phases of what you might call realism. For example, in 1947 I wrote my first poem, which has a peculiar title, *There's no Assortment Matthias.*[58] Here are some snippets from the end of it...

> And so today and from today on I can never ever again be rid of the urge to stroll with an Aramaic professor of laughter... Merry Silvester, today I can no longer be rid of the fissure in the brain, because to be siezed with rage, year-long happiness, joy... So I drown in sheer happiness, weddings and joys... Brethren, *l'art pour l'art* brethren, fair as *entartete Kunst*, true as the nightingale, perverted as the rose, without a fissure in the brain it really is impossible to live today. We cannot be deloused of liberty... Brethren...

Here you can see that just as I've had to do pirouettes on a postage stamp in life, I've done it in my texts as well, and go places where I don't even expect to find

[58] Published only in the Collected Works (Vol. 1, *Básnění* [Versifying, 1991]) as *Kolekce není. Mathias* (the difference is in the full-stop), consisting of the five separate poems: 'Jaro' (Spring), 'Léto' (Summer), 'Podzim' (Autumn), 'Zima' (Winter) and 'Věčný Silvestr' (Eternal Silvester; '[St] Silvester['s Day]' to the Czechs means New Year's Eve). 'Assortment' as in the title generally refers to a selection of biscuits intended to be hung on a Christmas tree.

myself... That's Klíma's ludibrionism for you, where everything arises from its opposite; it is the laughter of the gods of antiquity at how opposites stand juxtaposed; it is the melancholy relish of Otto Dix's[59] caricatures of how everything is dialectical.... at one point it's solemn, and right next to that it's comical... seeing one's wife dead – joy, madness, marriage...[60] for sale: white-haired puppies, baby rabbits, souvenir model chapels, Christmas decorations. Oh brethren... those are snippets from my poem *Spring, Summer, Autumn, Winter and Eternal Silvester*,[61] and there I suddenly reached the depths of my very self. But having reached or found my essence, I'd barely recovered when I would start writing again. I began adding metaphors, I was back again with that 'procreation in the Beautiful'. There I was, living in Nymburk, and in 1950 I discovered I couldn't live there any more. In short, I was too much the young gentleman, living at a brewery, doing all right, always nicely dressed, so I had to cut myself away from Nymburk. Hence I moved to Prague and there I lived and have lived until today; I was twenty-five years in Libeň. I rented an unfurnished room, the workshop of a former smithy at No. 24 Na hrázi; of course I live somewhere else now, but I was there for a quarter of a century. Me doing my pirouettes on a postage stamp. So I arrived there as a young gentleman, began commuting to Kladno and started

[59] Otto Dix (1891–1969), German expressionist painter and graphic artist who portrayed the negative aspects of human life. His portraits are grotesquely exaggerated caricatures.
[60] In the original, this sentence is in imitation of the language of Czech dream books.
[61] *Jaro, léto, podzim, zima a věčný Silvester*; see Note 58.

living a life you might call proletarian, and there it was that I wrote *Jarmilka*, my *Proprietress of the Foundry*,[62] I had to, because of the total realism[63] in which I was living. And so by cutting myself away, I wrote a total-realistic, fairly long story which comes close to good reportage, or the work of a Czech journalist, without metaphors, just a statement of what I'd seen at Kladno, and my heroine was just an ordinary girl, a tea-lady, and that's all. In other words these were the Fifties, and it was then that I worked my way to a sort of total realism. Of course, as the years went by, that environment bred in me certain associations, metaphors, and I began writing again as I used to write, but enriched; suddenly the lyricism of the small country town, those glorious sunsets, came back to me in the steelworks. I'd been writing total-realistically about what I saw, in the vicinity of those open-hearth furnaces, and it affected me just as stupendously as that young man had been affected as he walked with pretty girls along the riverbank, or went walking in the country and wrote poems. This time, there at Kladno in the Fifties, I wrote *Bambini di Praga* and *The Beautiful Steelworks*;[64] I was actually beginning to write literature that was more proletarian, while in my youth I had been inspired by the town and Ungaretti.[65] Though for me the pinnacle had been Apollinaire. Then suddenly, during the Fifties, I found

[62] The same story appears in various guises under the alternative titles of *Jarmilka* and *Majitelka hutí*.

[63] 'Total Realism' is Egon Bondy's term to describe a particular trend in the unofficial literature of the 1950s. On Bondy see Note 103.

[64] *Krásná Poldi*, meaning the Poldi Steelworks at Kladno.

[65] Giuseppe Ungaretti (1888–1970), leading Italian poet of the 'hermetic school' – so named by the critic Francesco Flora. See also Note 28.

my way to what Whitman, Sandburg,[66] Eliot in *The Wasteland*, and of course Joyce wrote about. For me Joyce was a real giant, and I am still reading him today. His *Ulysses* is another pinnacle for me; everything's there really. The whole of modern art is in *Ulysses*, which was written somewhere between 1912 and 1921, so all the art-forms – I mean Dadaism, Realism, Surrealism, the psychoanalytical, they all run through it; that current is even in Molly Bloom, it's the border area between the subconscious and consciousness, just about visible. So I was bewitched by Joyce and I would go so far as to say that to me he is the acme of literature, where poetry merges with prose, science, music. He was musical himself, with the 'Sirens' episode modelled on Richard Wagner's *Meistersinger*, written as a quintet.[67] Every episode of *Ulysses* has its own colour, its organ, its mode, its form, but taken together it constitutes a *gesamtkunstwerk*, and that for me is the acme. At Liběň I would often read the few pages of Joyce where Father Conmee explains to a class of school-children that Eternity is a mountain of sand, about as high as Mount Everest, and how once every hundred years a little bird comes and takes away one grain of sand and even after it has taken away that entire mountain of

[66] Carl Sandburg (1878–1967), American poet, in whose works enchantment with civilization mingles with bitterness at the hardness of life and hope for the ideal socialist society.

[67] Joyce himself referred to 'Sirens' as being made up of 'all the parts of a *fuga per canonem*'. The entire section is replete with musical allusion, metaphor and quotation. For a lucid exposition of all, including the less obvious or genuinely obscure, sources used by Joyce in this 'prelude and fugue' see James Joyce: *Ulysses*, edited with an Introduction by Jeri Johnson, Oxford etc., 1993 (World's Classics edition), pp. 874–82. That analysis reveals only one Wagnerian dimension, namely a passing allusion to *Das Rheingold*.

sand Eternity will still not have begun. I have deduced that humour and a sense for the tragic in life are twins, two roads leading out of the same valley, and that a dour drama in the end reveals the same essence as trivial slapstick. I have derived from whisky and soda the rhythmical alternation of those two pitches; I have alternated the cold current with the hot, which Babel was so good at, juxtaposing a diamond and gonorrhoea in the same text. If I could now, from the perspective of a man who is seventy, do a cutting job on all that I have written so far, I would take my scissors and assemble something not unlike another *Ulysses*, because I too see myself as one who, like Odysseus, was drawn into war against his will. I also took part in the war as a dispatcher against my will. Like Joyce I love music, thanks to Rabelais I like quoting others, just as Joyce did, and if I could, I can see sections that I could cut out of my books and I'd be truly blessed if I made up a book which would be like *Ulysses*, or failing that like *A Portrait of the Artist as a Young Man*. A one-of-these-days event, but wedded to myth...

And when do you intend to do it?

I've only just had the idea. I always think of things ex post, when I look back on them. What I've just said I was saying for the first time in my life.

Whenever I talk about you to my friends, we always arrive at Robert Musil and James Joyce. Via Uncle Pepin, via those who would like to step on their own shadows, you are reporting on the fate of that Czech Bloom.

Maybe. This country has seen the publication of

Portrait..., then *Ulysses* and *Anna Livia Plurabella*, and *Dubliners...*

Portrait *is associated with the concept of 'epiphany'. I would suggest that your current literary persona is also rooted in your human essence and in that constant metamorphosing: having been through phases of realism and grand poetry you have now arrived at Magical Realism.*

Perhaps. I always start out from an event, and an event is precisely where you find that Magical Realism. Where reality is also suddenly fantastical, where the reality I have lived, precisely thanks to my mobility and my rummaging after artificial destinies, thanks to those crazy romantic jobs I've had, often displays, or provides the arena for, a reality that approximates almost to fiction, or a kind of legend. I manufacture legends about myself. The legend always starts out from reality. But from the way I apprehend reality, or a fact, what suddenly emerges is, thanks to my *pábení*,[68] a fiction. So I twist the end back to front and simply round it off somehow and make it an integral whole, and then something like a drop of water – the real story – emerges, though it still needs touching up, otherwise it would be just reportage. Literature, or that which is inside me, keeps forcing me to change

---

[68] *Pábení*, though not Hrabal's invention, is an expression now most intimately associated with him. It is not recorded in any dictionary, but one attempt to define it says: 'The *pábitel* looks for poetry in everyday reality..., he defends himself against uglified phraseology and the mannerism of forms of communication. He amuses us and grabs our attention with his entirely fresh, unhackneyed way of seeing things.' (Radko Pytlík on *Ostře sledované vlaky*, in the Afterword to Bohumil Hrabal: *Tři novely* [Three Novelle], Prague 1989, p. 326.) The expression has been translated elsewhere as 'palavering'.

things a bit, to make little improvements, even to give it a special kind of sense or peculiarity, in other words to give me a bit of fun at the same time, and the having fun is that ludibrionism we've mentioned. In other words, I have to shift it in a slightly different direction, which is what turns my narrative, my tale into a literary story... As you know, my literary forms are not usually of the grand kind, either they're poems or picaresque novels, or at most ballads or novelle, like *Closely Observed Trains*,[69] but there always has to be some kind of catharsis. Though with me catharsis is not programmatic, or *à la thèse*, it just springs from that playfulness, even if things turn out badly, as in *Closely Observed Trains*. None the less, I did have to end it as I did, that is, as a work of art or something akin to one, what Shklovskii[70] calls a particularization, in other words I particularized not only the narrative mode, but also the structure, by executing a pirouette on a postage stamp...

The novella Closely Observed Trains *may well be a paradox, but it did also spring from playfulness, since in this case playfulness is the method.*

It was odd. First I just made notes, they came out in *Buds*.[71] They are just meetings and visits. I used to visit the station-master at Nymburk and he loved listening

---

[69] *Ostře sledované vlaky* (1965); this extremely popular novella and film has gone under various English titles – *Closely Watched Trains*, *Closely Observed Trains*, *A Close Watch on the Trains*.

[70] Viktor Borisovich Shklovskii (1893–1984), Russian writer and literary theorist, founder of Formalism.

[71] *Poupata* (1970). This first Prague edition was not put on sale, and most of the printing was pulped. The book was subsequently published in Cologne in 1982.

to my yarns about my experiences during the war and the Protectorate, when I'd been a truant at Dobrovice and a train-dispatcher at Kostomlaty near Nymburk. And everybody who listened was entranced by my narration, my slightly ridiculous narration. Like about the station-master and his pigeons, when the station-master was expecting promotion and then the Director arrives and he appears all covered in pigeon-shit. Everyone, the dispatcher, the station-master, all of them, when they heard stories about someone else, about the station-master at Dobrovice, they were struck speechless. Because they were suddenly living it – what if it had happened to them, how distraught they would have been, much as he was. I didn't pick up those motifs, those notes, until about ten years later and then wrote *Closely Observed Trains*. And I would say that was my first manuscript, manuscript in the sense that I realized that what I was about to write was not *à la thèse*, no mere banality of mine. Roland Barthes has said that a manuscript is an act of historical solidarity, meaning that this was the first time I reckoned with a reader, or many readers, or that I conceived it as a kind of message. What I had written before had been just for me. *Closely Observed Trains* is my first manuscript, my first committed literature, because it had suddenly dawned on me that my story was not just mine but that of several, maybe even millions of people who had been involved in the war or had had to live during the Protectorate here. And not only here, but in Hungary, Poland, Russia and elsewhere, at the fronts; so I wrote, consciously I wrote it as a manuscript, and not as a highly subjective statement. I now reckoned with the reader and by now I could sense what impact it might have on a reader and what I would perhaps be telling him in order to strike a chord in him, or to tell him that even ordinary, ludicrous people can be heroes. To my mind, the apparently last are first.

Apart from irony and the grotesque, it is this same way of looking at ordinary, ludicrous people that links you to the Hungarian writer, Örkény. The Tóth Family *and* Closely Observed Trains *spring from a common source.*

There's much truth in that. My view of people does link me distantly to Örkény,[72] who has roughly the same poetics, as I could see from the Drama Club[73] performance of *The Tóths*. More or less the same as I have in *Closely Observed Trains*. But I have only seen it; I haven't read his novels. I've only read the mini-stories.[74] How they had me falling about laughing! It's a glorious little book, like that little prose-work of Baudelaire's.[75] When I saw Örkény on stage, it was suddenly brought home to me that here was a writer of

[72] István Örkény (1912–79), Hungarian writer and dramatist. Two of his plays have been performed in Britain: *Macskajáték* (*Catsplay*, 1966) at Greenwich and *Tóték* (*The Tóth Family*, 1967) at the Traverse Theatre, Glasgow, in the 1970s.

[73] Činoherný klub, a small progressive and experimental theatre in Prague.

[74] Referring to Örkény's *Egyperces novellák* (*One-Minute Stories*; various collections appeared at various times), a genre of Örkény's own invention, surrealistic and full of black humour. The Hungarian authorities viewed this experimental literature as particularly worth disseminating: a selection was published in German and English translation (Budapest: Kossuth, 1992; various translators) and left *gratis* in the bedrooms of the main tourist hotels. Another selection of *One-Minute Stories* (trans. Judith Sollosy) is also available in English (Budapest, 1995, 1996, in cooperation with Brandl & Schlesinger, Sydney).

[75] Presumably the *Petits poèmes en prose*.

the same water, but I didn't know he was my age, even older. I knew he'd talked about me when he was in Prague. I heard that he gave a lecture at the Writers' Union, a sort of talk where he mentioned me frequently. He would have liked to meet me, but I happened to be away somewhere. His wife, who came and spent some time here and saw my *Tender Barbarian*[76] at the Drama Club, said, I quote: 'It's a pity my husband couldn't see it, because those two people, without ever meeting or seeing each other, share the same poetics.' I felt honoured that Mr Örkény wished to meet me. Unfortunately it never came about. Mrs Örkény said that his and my poetics were akin... Pirouettes on a postage stamp, it occurs to me.

One of Örkény's thoughts might have come from your lips: 'The nation will have matured when it learns to laugh at itself, and also to laugh at things which would once have made it weep and were horrendous.' You say roughly the same. Örkény wrote a grotesque comedy called The Key-Seekers,[77] *about how we don't admit our own failures to ourselves, even describing those failures as successes.*

The realization of defeat is the beginning of triumph. But the world is nothing but one triumph after another, and people do nothing but keep triumphing, just like after car crashes the world over, it was always the other chap's fault, never mine. My triumph begins when I admit to disasters that haven't befallen me, I accept the blame for crashes I haven't caused, and so

[76] *Něžný barbar* (Prague [samizdat], 1974; Cologne [emigré edition], 1981; Prague, 1990).
[77] *Kulcskeresok* (1976).

all defeats are my victories. The most beautiful sickness on earth is health. Most people feel so lousy that the opposite condition is the exception. You must be very, very ill in order to be well afterwards. And to afford yourself the luxury of... writing.

You might find it a bit odd, but for me the identity of Örkény's texts with real life was confirmed by one thing that happened to him: 'With the exception of my parents I have never wept over anyone. There was a time when I was on the brink of tears for thirty seconds – in Los Angeles, where my hosts took me by car to the coast. The city is criss-crossed by endless highways: cars stream six lanes one way, six lanes the other. Suddenly I saw a lonely blind man standing there, wanting to cross. He stood there with his stick, tapping on the roadway and waiting for help. But you can drive for hours on end before seeing a pedestrian. I don't know how long he'd been waiting there, or long he waited after; all I know is that he was waiting pointlessly, since stopping on those highways is prohibited. It was a twentieth-century trap, and it made my eyes well up.' There is an identity between your works and your life as well.

I try hard to make sure there is. Wherever I have been a let-down as a person, my heroes are let-downs as well. And the things I'm proud of – and they're just ordinary human trivia – those are the things my heroes are also proud of. Whenever I've written anything, I've always tried to start from things as they are, not as they should be. I've never had a pre-set programme, like, say, humanism. Fine thing that that may be, I always oppose it with hominism; you know, a story of an ordinary person, the events in his life, no trying to project myself into humanism, or some grand idea, erecting a hero to act in the name of

Something Big, as if he knew... No, just an ordinary person who may well do things like that, but with no grand gestures, no great euphoria. My heroes, if they ever are euphoric, are euphoric in the name of hominism, that is, the life of ordinary people. It even seems to me – and this is something else I've learnt – that a writer should be humble, and live more or less like other folk. He shouldn't entertain too high expectations; for a certain period – ideally right through life – he should have no luxuries. I cut myself away from those five rooms, the brewery. Whether consciously or subconsciously – it doesn't matter – I knew that that was how my ancestors had begun. When my grandparents married, what did they have? Grandmother had an alarm-clock to get up on time, and grandfather had a half-litre beer-glass. That's how I began too. It's all about a kind of ordinariness, suppressing one's self in the sense of not being surrounded by a degree of luxury and a book-case and central heating and stuff like that. I could have had these things, but I've always dispensed with them. I could be called well-off, but I spend most of my time in Kersko, at my cottage, where my only access to water is by having a pump. I do have a pump and I have to carry all my water in buckets, like ordinary people. It's not the way they do things nowadays: nowadays people have got flush toilets and suchlike. But I keep to the old ways, everything by touching and sensing. Everything proceeds through me: I see the water, I do the pumping, and I do the fetching and carrying in buckets. That might all seem very trivial, but it's what keeps me alive. Mark you, I'm an admirer of the elemental. I love making fires – I can have five stoves on the go at once; nothing makes me happier. That was Libeň for you, where I did have stoves, and an outside toilet, and when it snowed even my wife would go through the falling snow to the toilet outside. Our heating was the stoves. We used to have a huge jug which we took to the pub to get filled with beer. I lived simply with ordinary people who would speak to me in the street; some called me Bohoušek, some addressed me as Doctor, but I was one of them, and it was an honour to live among them. It's always been my impression that ordinary people live much more intensely: people who keep rabbits, people who know how to hoe their own potatoes, go to their local, people who live quite ordinary lives; these folk get much more out of life than intellectuals. In other words, even in writing it's been my endeavour to suppress the intellectual overlay. Conversely, the man down below, the one almost at the bottom of the social scale, for me he's the pinnacle; people like that have always taught me far more about life than any intellectual. In the ordinary way, an intellectual merely knows things, whereas the common man has experienced them profoundly, and experience, that's the point from which I sail off on my voyage. As I told you earlier on, there was a whole period when I called myself a recorder, a recorder of the events ordinary people tell me; not like now, as we sit in front of a tape-recorder, no. Say I've known someone down at the pub for ten or a dozen years. Suddenly, as if triggered by the given moment or situation, your ordinary person says something, perhaps just as we're setting off home. So an old chap might say: 'The only body fit for the grave is one that's past it.' Or a beer-waitress might suddenly let out a mournful: 'A city full of people, yet I'm all on my little lonesome!' It's as if you were to carve it somewhere on me with a knife; I've simply got it tattooed and I don't need to write anything down, because these stories, they stick in my memory. And these are my building-blocks, or the driving force of my writing. So when I'm full, when my head's like a two-year-old cabbage, when it's fit to burst, that's when the law of super-pressure actually kicks in. I have to find the moment when I suddenly have an image of the whole, of the bed-sheet in which it's all lying; then I just sit down and spew it all out compulsively, as it comes, onto the typewriter, and there it is. Previously I would play about with it, cutting it up, pasting it together; you could say that half of my things, including *Closely Observed Trains*, are not only cut-and-pasted, but rewritten say five or six times over. Now, as an elderly gent, I've indulged myself by writing several whole books off the cuff. Or I've made three variants, then chosen the one I liked best; but take something like *I Served the King of England*,[78] that was written *alla prima*. I wrote it up on the roof; for eighteen days no one came and I just wrote down everything I knew, and because I live in pubs it was things I knew from others... I got the opening from the publican at the Blue Star in Sadská.[79]

---

[78] *Jak jsem obsluhoval anglického krále* (Cologne, 1980); later editions as *Obsluhoval jsem anglického krále* (Prague, 1990).
[79] A small town about 20 miles East of Prague.

And where did you write it?

Kersko. And after I read it through I said to myself: there's no more needs doing to this; it's all there. That's quite rare for me. But if you take *Pábitelé*, the short-stories, well, it might not look like it, but I cut them about and rewrote them time and time again, just looking for that final stage when the paragraphs would fit together and it would look like an organic whole with its own rhyme and reason.

From what you've said, you have tried to style your life in such a way as to preserve your identity, the identity between your heroes and you. But most of your heroes are afflicted with a curse, and you too have been not far removed from the poètes maudits.

Well, the curse is really on those down below, in the ale-houses, people who no longer have anyone or anywhere else to go but the pub. And there they are in contact with the *poètes maudits*, and if ever I were to try and tell them about how Verlaine or Baudelaire lived, they would be touched. And suddenly my heaven, my intellectual firmament, connects with even the lowest. And that too is, I believe, what makes Baudelaire so great – his profound compassion. He had that black girl, Mlle Duval, didn't he? He was capable of noticing those poor street-girls, just like all the Impressionist painters who came after him. *Les Fleurs du Mal* and *Petits poèmes en Prose*, that's where you'll find it; he could combine intellectual spleen and the banality of everyday life; which is what became the essence of Impressionist painting. The Impressionists: it might look like sheer banality, but it's a celebration. Streets, whores, a portrait of some woman, a landscape of the sort any-

one might see, the Seine beyond Paris, the Paris bou-
levards; and by that stage they knew how to record
what are called the masses. That tide of people. Impressionism ends at the turn of the century, and the
streets are no longer just a story in colours, but a kind
of ominous mass, capable of hurling things down and
breaking things up and overturning not only the whole
city, but the entire order. Late Impressionist works
speak of the masses as a threat, as indeed they became
in 1917 in Russia, and anywhere else where the people
today called, rather nastily, the masses, have bur-
geoned. Though it's really a coexistence of people.
After all, every man has his name and surname and
destiny.

*Since you have such fellow-feeling with the damned, I expect you
also know in what respect you are accursed,* maudit, *yourself,
don't you?*

I never actually have been. Even if you've got cares
of the heart or you've got to do to something you'd
prefer not to, it doesn't mean there's a curse on you. I
expect it's because I wasn't destined to become accursed. But fellow-feeling, as I have learned myself
ever since childhood, and later from Schopenhauer – I
am assailed by it, by compassion, the moment I see a
man who *is* accursed. I reckon there's no shortage of
such types as I've tried to portray in my short-stories.
Even Jarmilka[80] ought perhaps to be accursed. But she
isn't; she's even a Virgin Mary; the man doesn't want
her because she's pregnant, everyone pokes fun at her,

[80] See note 62.

but she's aglow with something like – not happiness, but that blessedness of the poor in spirit. There's something in her like on the tympanum of a cathedral. There you always find those who are blessed. Those no longer affected by birth, or death, or torment, and who are actually unfathomably happy in this world. Even their life can sometimes evoke envy, since these people don't suffer from spleen. I have always suffered from spleen, or profound melancholy, but melancholy, as Jaspers[81] tells us, is a borderline category, like any mood is a borderline category. That particular mood is extremely fruitful because although you're alone, it's a kind of sparky solitude, and you could even say – after all, you hear others say it – that it is sought after, even induced artificially by alcohol precisely to help you suffer from spleen and be melancholic – because in that condition you're most amenable to what he calls 'solid revelation'. Suddenly something just turns up, you get an idea that you could have expected only in that state of melancholy. In a state of hip-hip-hooray and tickety-boo, in any excess of joy, you'd never get that particular idea. It has to be in a state of quietude, in the depths of melancholy. Leibniz's dictum about the melancholy of the eternal structure is my basic tenet. I know I'll die in melancholy, I know that one day, in profound melancholy, even the starry sky will fall in, yet there are also moments when I suddenly feel that eternity does endure and that I am; that sometimes I even am who I am. What Moses was told by God. But that happens

[81] Karl Jaspers (1883–1969), German philosopher (of Existentialism) and psychiatrist; a humanist opposed to the reunification of Germany (claiming that united Germany is always imperialist in a Prussian militarist manner).

to us only a once or twice in a lifetime. Dostoyevsky says that when he had an epileptic fit that didn't last long – fifteen seconds – he seemed to see what Breton sought, that glass house where everything is under glass, where the staircase is glass, the walls are glass, the bed is glass, and he is lying there and covering himself with a glass sheet on which, sooner or later, appears, incised with a diamond: *Who am I?* You could say that even writing is an enquiry into who one is; you never know. And if you do, you're a genius; even young people can be affected like that. The prose-writer will discover it through the entire writing process and maybe he'll behold it only a few minutes before he dies, but he is ever on the alert, like Zen Buddhists. And what does a Zen Buddhist do? He meditates, reads, meditates and watches out for that one sentence to appear. And when the sentence does come, his heaven is preserved, and he cures himself with that sentence and resurrects others. It is the mainstay of that particular vault. In other words, you can see that even my writing is a constant pursuit of my final definition of my own self, an enquiry after whether I have ever been an identity, like the two matching halves of the Koh-i-Noor 'Waldes' patent press-stud.[82] Even you are an identity, but straightaway you're split in two again; *kein Objekt ohne Subjekt*. You're back rattling around again, back with Kant; there is no *Ding an sich selbst*, and if there is, you arrive at it like at the Platonic idea, like Kierkegaard, in a single leap, like Christian-

[82] The reference is to the Koh-i-Noor company, once a major Czech producer and exporter of small items of stationery and haberdashery – pencils, paperclips, press-studs etc. The logo was a winking press-stud face.

ity, by the odd miracle or even via the past. A writer also has it; in a sense writing is raising questions via others, invocation. I am much given to quoting what others have said. When I share their identity that way, I am agreeing with them, but I keep on asking about myself and my mission, and by asking about my own mission I am simultaneously asking about the mission of those about me, my fellow-citizens. Sometimes it's also the mission of literature to ask after the fate of people the world over. That gift was granted to such geniuses as Dostoyevsky, or Bruno Schulz, or Isaak Babel, or Hemingway, or Walt Whitman, who inspire young lads in Africa and Japan and goodness knows where else. Yet they are stories written in quite a different milieu, some from Russia, others from America, yet others from France. The ancient Chinese died out long ago, yet only now, in this half of the twentieth century, do we find Lao Tzu inspiring Henry Miller. Only now have Lao Tzu's writings become intelligible, because the crisis the world is in has so matured that we suddenly understand the *Canonical Book of Virtues*, and so we understand Lao Tzu himself, who left China in the sixth century to disappear somewhere in India because he felt that the society and order in the country where he lived didn't fit in with his ideas and with what he'd learnt from the ancients. That's also an answer to the question of identity, my identity as well, since I think that I too have sought to discover in others who I am; and that's probably why I get such a kick out of communicating with others. It follows, I think, from what I've been saying that I'm at my happiest when I'm communicating. It's my defence against *ennui* and spleen. Communication is the bottleneck through which I gargle my way to other people. I'm quite up to being – have been ever since a child – in communication with my cats, because it's so easy to reach the feline soul, and win it over, and make friends with cats the same way as with people. And I know the cats count on me; I've had them with me in Kersko for fifteen years and they wait patiently for me to turn up just to see them. If it's snowing and been raining for some time, I have to go and see them, because they are my friends. I have to give them some milk and meat, but when I arrive, they refuse to eat – they want me to fondle them, they've been waiting for a few warm human words. That's the kind of communication that for me symbolizes my relation to the rest of the natural world. To me all seasons are beautiful because I am in love with Nature, I am pregnant by Her...

What god do you believe in?

Definitely not a person-like god. My god is in me. Not that he *is* Bohumil Hrabal, but inside my soul I have a literal sense of kinship with something; a sense that, somewhere inside, there's a spot which is capable of communicating with something higher than me, something that has a higher charge, something transcendental that always tends to the metaphysical. In other words it's the kind of Good that achieves such slight progress in the world, yet everyone believes in it. And this Good, and the slight step forward that it takes – I sense, and not just me, others too sense it, that this step is God. God is always good, I think. Though there is the problem of why he also uses evil.

But of course it's just light and shade, everything has its opposite, and it's only the synthesis of such opposites that smacks of something that we call God. To put it differently, for me it's what we have in Christ and above all in Lao Tzu; it is a path. And as I proceed along that path I do register when I have met Good, and conversely when I have been abandoned by it. But I'm in earnest pursuit of it all the time; that search is an endless journey leading to something that we call the light. My god is my native tongue. The word...

Don't you like the shade?

No. I love the dark, but I don't like shade. I go out in the street and the sun's shining, and I walk so as to be always in the sun. Even when it's hot, forty degrees, I get out of the shade to walk in the sun. I don't know. It's been with me since childhood. Wherever the sun doesn't go I don't go either. Except to the pub.

And you love darkness.

And I love the dark, not a murky darkness of course, but a glorious starlit night, even a glorious night when it's raining, when...

So you don't mean dark. You mean a purity, a self-purification.

Yes, you could say that. If I had to be in a murky dark I'd go mad. But then – I do like being afraid...

You're not talking about darkness now, but about something wonderful.

That's right. Actually about the night; darkness frightens me. But I enjoy being afraid.

Eliot also disliked the dark, and he also liked cats. You have said that when you wanted to do some reading as a child you had cats around you. – In Hungary a miscellany has been published in which numerous writers – of prose and verse, and including Eliot – write of their relationship with cats. How did you view cats when you were young, and how do you see them now?

I don't think I have ever been so devoted to a mistress as I have to my cats. With them I experience a shocking syndrome of lovers...

When did that great love begin?

As I remember it, I was on my way from school in Nymburk one day and suddenly something let out a miaow in the grapevine beneath some windows, and there I saw this kitten. It had a pink nose, with white bits under its chin and on its paws; otherwise it was a tabby. All I know is that it was pitiful, and, as I stood there amazed, it clung to me and I discovered something I'd never known before. Suddenly I was being tender and at that very moment I knew that this kitten must never leave me, and it nestled up to me and I won the battle to have the kitten stay with us. It used to sleep with me, and whenever I suddenly missed him in the hours before dawn I would go out as I was, in my nightshirt, and call out across the meadow, and he'd always come running by leaps and bounds from the direction of the malthouse and I'd clutch him to me, and he'd be wet and smell of grass. Then we'd lie together on the bed, the cat stretched out beside me, and I would take great care not to smother him; our faces would be close together. One day I went to the cinema; they were showing slapstick comedies and one was called *Serpentine the Bricklayer*, I have a vague recollection it was Lupino Lane,[83] and my little tom-cat came to be called Serpentýn.

Are you still as fond of cats?

Every morning I have to drive out to Kersko to see my cats, watch over them, feed them. And when the weather's nasty, to lift their spirits. Obviously, I also do some writing while I'm there, and they sit and watch me, while my wife bellows that I've got the Mahler turned up too loud. I've got two cats, one called Pepito and one called Pusinka. They sigh sweetly and listen to Mahler's symphonies, the sixth, the tenth, then they sigh even more, and then they sleep, and sigh sweetly even in their sleep. Of course, anyone who keeps cats, take note: I'm also a bit of a husbandman. The time comes around when someone has to kill the kittens. Ever since I was a teenager it was me who did it. Precisely because I loved them, lived with them and knew there could be no question of their remaining alive, it was me who would put them down. It was also me who, last year or the year before that, had to dispatch two cats because I had twelve of them altogether. Two had to go. They had to be shot, by me, so there would be fewer of them. But there's less of me too...

---

[83] Hrabal's recollection of 'Serpentýn zedník' is at this point indeed vague. The film in question is French, *Serpentin manoeuvre* (1919, dir. Jean Durand [1882–1946], prod. Serge Sandberg [1879–1981]), one of eight Serpentin titles in which the hero was played by Marcel Lévesque (1879–1981). See http://us.imdb.com/title/tt0493878/-fullcredits. In consequence of Hrabal's vague recollection Lévesque does not appear in the 'Index of Names' to Hrabal's oeuvre in Vol. 19 of the Collected Works edition (pp. 115–54), being represented, perforce, under 'Lane, Lupino' (p. 135).

Did you do it out of compassion?

Well, what could I do with twelve cats? It's not on.
You have to be like a husbandman who has a farm and
knows when to kill what. It has to be the father. We all
like steak, so there has to be someone who is lord of the
killing, the butcher. If you want the home to be at least
half-harmonious, you can't have fifteen cats in it. Let
alone in a house in the woods. Even two cats can drive
you mad, when one has kittens and starts bringing baby
rabbits indoors. At that stage you don't know whose
side you're on. The rabbits' or the cat's. Sometimes it
makes you so mad that if you had a gun in the house
you'd shoot the wretched cat no matter what. Because
the baby rabbits the cats catch are so much prettier and
sweeter than any damn' cat of mine. So there you have
it, Mr Hrabal also has to know how to be ruthless,
though at some cost to himself. I wrote a book about it,
named after a cat that had to be destroyed. That novella is called *Mo-mo*,[84] and I wrote it as an indictment of
myself for a crime almost against humanity. Because
having had to kill two cats, I'd seen that just as you
can't kill a cat with impunity, in the broader picture the
same goes for killing a man. We live in an age when – I
heard this on Radio Vienna – since the end of the war,
meaning from 1945 to date, no fewer than twenty-one
million more people have died fighting somewhere.
Whether fighting for a better tomorrow or out of brutality, it doesn't matter. Twenty-one million people have
been killed, and here am I going to pieces over having
to kill a couple of cats to preserve my domestic har-

[84] That is, 'Little Car' (as 'Autíčko' in *Život bez smokingu* [Life without a dinner-
jacket], 1986).

78

mony. Because cats that are out of harmony with the home will give you the same hell as when you have two mistresses who come to see your wife and have it all out. So it's better to dispatch the wife or mistress humanely, at least in the mind. But I had to kill the cats, and that's an indictment not just of me, but of the whole world, since I wrote it up as the case for the prosecution against myself. It's a ballad. Once more I achieved – as I put it in connection with *Jarmilka* – total realism. It may have a literary form, but like an honest journalist I'd written a reportage on what happened to me. We had an almost fatal accident, which I later saw as retribution. Our Ford Escort crashed head-on, but miraculously we survived. Catharsis and my heaven.

Was it you driving?

No, my wife. But I was happy for the sense of retribution it gave me for personally causing the death of two dear cats. I feel that in the message of that novella, in that communication, I had crossed some line, that borderline where things cease to be literature.

And what is transcendence, Mr Hrabal?

That won't help you. All great lovers – even in Dostoyevsky – have come close to killing their beloved. And I loved those cats, but some of them had to go – it was them or me. I couldn't stand the racket any more. All great writers know this and have run into the problem; so has almost every man. Just as Livy, who wrote the history of the world, writes that he's never met anyone who wouldn't like to commit suicide, I've certainly not met anyone who wouldn't like to dispatch some cherished creature. But it is only ever played out in words, like 'I could kill you' or 'I could shoot all those cats', whereas I actually did it. So what's the difference between the conditional 'I could do it' and the indicative 'I did it'. According to Christ, whosoever covets his neighbour's wife, that is, if you want to shag her, as we put it, then you've already had sex with her in your heart. Light on the horizon...

And that's a sin.

Yes, in my view too. I am a cat-lover, but when the time comes, well, ever since I was twelve it's always been up to me either to drown the kittens, or bash their heads on the concrete to kill them; me – my mother would have gone mad. All I know is that I felt dreadful at having done something awful; the blood always rushes to my head when I think about it and I have a sense of having been guilty of a crime ever since those childhood days. It had to be done and I did it. Because I loved them and still do... cats.

What other crimes do you have on your conscience?

Well, sometimes I... What's the difference between you killing or someone killing you? Sometimes, when you think back to when you hurt some young woman, you just weren't interested in her and left her, then she wrote and begged you time and again to let her be with you, and you didn't have ears to hear – in a sense that's also murder, psychological murder. But those are the problems we run into, the other side of my ludibrionism, my *pábení* of melancholy, my hominism – not humanism – so that I too can, and sometimes must, be cruel. But I'm generally ruthless with myself as well. I never make things easy for myself and even magnify my guilt complex. When something awful happens somewhere in the world I even take it as if it was something I'd done, or something done to me. All those great massacres, everything that happens, it's me. That's what Schopenhauer taught me, and he was taught by Indian philosophy. I see people shooting each other in the back, in war, the innocent ones, and that's me. And even that cat, the killed cat, that's me. If I see a dog that's been run over, that's me; or that profound fellow-feeling. Compassion can sometimes lead us to keep cats alive when they're almost dead from neglect, abandoned, scrawny. But wouldn't it be more humane to shoot them? When you think about it... And so help them pass to the other side. That too can befall one who calls himself a lover; but anyway, what I experience with cats, how we understand one another, that doesn't exist any more...

Remind me of their names...

Pepito, the tabby tom, and Pusinka, he's the ginger one. He's a real Pussy, like Real Madrid are Pussies.[85]

[85] This is a slightly tricky passage to translate: I have retained the second cat's Czech name and picked it up allusively with the word 'pussy' as essentially encapsulating the 'sweet' side of cats in English. However, the primary meaning of Cz. *pusinka* is 'kiss'; its secondary meaning is 'meringue'. This looks back to French *baiser*, both 'kiss' and 'meringue'. German and Polish have merely *borrowed* the French word (as Ger. *Baiser* and Pol. *beza*) for 'meringue', while Czech has *translated* the French and given *pusinka* both its French meanings. The uninitiated might not appreciate that one of the several nicknames of Real Madrid is *Los Merengues*, i.e. 'meringues', not, perhaps, an ideal name for a cat in English (sweet though the connotations must be), hence the problem.

Are they different?

Chalk and cheese! Completely opposite characters. Pusinka's always elegant, eats slowly, and is *zuckersüss*, coy, in all he does. Pepito loves his food, never stops screeching, keeps calling us, and everything he does is based on noise. His eating's more like guzzling and he's quite shamelessly fond of being pampered, while Pusinka is, well, sort of prim. – And it's right and proper that if I love animals, I can't have fifteen of them. They start going mad. They get so jealous! I once had six or nine – they can turn one small flat into hell. *Inferno con Paradiso*.

And you made a psychological issue of it, killing a cat...

No less than Dostoyevsky.

In Tender Barbarian *you wrote that Vladimír's[86] sickness equated with health. In that case the same applies to you.*

Wait, back a minute. Dostoyevsky did it as an intellectual and used Raskolnikov to investigate whether he could stand it. Two women, nothing to write home about, no good for anything in particular, so that if he kills them not much will come of it. In other words, he was investigating the issue of moral conscience and the conscience of that *Weltgefühl*, *Welthafte*, true. Whereas I killed because I had no option, with the cats going crazy in their own company and driving me crazy as well; this cat-love nearly did for me and either I would

[86] This and later references to 'Vladimír' mean Vladimír Boudník (1924–68), experimental Czech painter and graphic artist of 'lyrical abstraction'; Hrabal's 'tender barbarian'. See Martin Pilář: 'Hrabal and Boudník: a fateful friendship', in David Short (ed.): *Bohumil Hrabal (1914–97): Papers from a Symposium* (London, 2004), pp. 51–58.

have hanged myself or one of them had to go. It was an issue which I regularly observe in farmers, people who live in the country and who I think are incredibly cruel to animals, but that's how it has to be. The farmer's dog has to be chained up, and there can only be as many cats as he can pour milk for or enough to catch all his mice, but the rest have to go. That's how I stand, as a farmer who wants a measure of harmony in the house among the animals that live there. But someone has to be Lord of the Killing.

What do you think – did Dostoyevsky kill?

Dostoyevsky was certainly never far off killing someone, and the motif does turn up in his writing, and always, in the nick of time... or he does kill! We've got Raskolnikov, we've got Stavrogin, and you might say that it's all him in these characters; all the devils that haunted him are in them; his holy sickness is in them. And in Karamazov too! There Dostoyevsky's is a divided self. He is at once Alyosha, the intellectual Ivan and the spontaneous Mitya. And at the same time he's the old lecher, Karamazov.

And I think he's also the harlot, Grushenka!

Grushenka! I wonder, Grushenka. Mind you, she's a saint! Dostoyevsky's women are the salvation of his men. And in Russia generally, they've all got women by their sides who save them. 'Mitya, my life!'[87]

---

[87] This 'quotation' may be a bit of Hrabalesque mystification, or just another failing of memory. Nowhere in *The Brothers Karamazov* does it actually occur, though at one point in Chapter 3 Mitya, kneeling and holding Grusha in his arms, does say 'Grusha, my life [...]'.

Do they save you too?

I can't say I've ever noticed. It's more men who save me. You see I have loved too much; four times I've been very much in love and wanted nothing more than to marry the girl I loved until death do us part. I used to fall terribly in love, four times in total,[88] and each time it lasted four years, even my inglorious jobs lasted four years; four years at Kladno, four years in the theatre, four years recycling paper, and four years on the railways. But the way I loved each of the – more erotic – objects of my affection, I was like that playing-card with a picture of a bear-leader and his bear, which has a ring in its nose; the bear, that was me. And I always wanted to get married, but the targets of my affection all took the view that I wasn't cut out for marriage; I was too dreamy, and then I spent more than I earned, so the idea always sort of fell by the wayside; thus it was more me who was abandoned. And I would start going to pieces, going to pieces...

I expect that's why you write less about women than men.

Or the very reason why I should. Now of all times...! Listen. Take *Cutting it Short*,[89] narrated by my

[88] This doubtless refers to the first four main women in Hrabal's life: Jiřina Sokolová, Olina Micková, Blanka Krauseová and Eliška Plevová (Pipsi), each of whom had an impact on his writing. As did the later April Gifford, the eponymous addressee of *Dopisy Dubence* (Letters to April). (On the latter see Pavel Janáček: 'Hrabal's *Listopadový uragán* in the context of the "November Revolution" as a literary theme', in *Bohumil Hrabal (1914–97)*, pp. 105–18; for a view of Pipsi's role in Hrabal's writing see Robert Pynsent: 'Hrabal's Autobiographical Trilogy', *ibid.*, pp. 97–104.)

[89] *Postřižiny* (Prague [samizdat], 1974; Prague, 1976); English translation (James Naughton) together with *The Little Town Where Time Stood Still* (London, New York, 1993).

mother; the trilogy[90] I'm working on now is told with great mirth by my wife. There are manuscripts by women talking about their menfolk. One talks about Picasso,[91] another about Tolstoy,[92] yet another about Dostoyevsky. Mme Dostoyevsky talking about her husband.[93] But it strikes me that these women defend their men too hard and stylise them too much in the direction of greatness, as artists and as men. I concluded that I'd let my wife do the talking back-to-front. Part 1 is written and I've just finished Part 2, where my wife talks about me, but she's inclined to keep knocking me and showing up my negative sides. Male affectations are something awful!

So do you write fact or fiction?

Not fiction, more the truth. Mind you, everything is truth.

And what has appeared so far?

Nothing yet. I've got Part 3 more or less sketched out, but it's my wife talking about me and putting me

---

[90] Referring to *Proluky* (Vacant lots, published by various emigré houses in Toronto, Purley and Cologne, 1986; Prague, 1991), *Svatby v domě* (Weddings in the House, Toronto, 1987; Prague, 1991) and *Vita Nuova* (Toronto, 1987; Prague, 1991). This trilogy earned Hrabal the Jaroslav Seifert literary prize. See Pynsent: 'Hrabal's autobiographical trilogy' (note 88).

[91] Françoise Gilot: *Life with Picasso*, New York,1964; *Vivre avec Picasso*, Paris, 1974.

[92] It may be conjectured that this refers to the memoirs of Natalya Vasilyevna Krandiyevskaja-Tolstaja, on Alexej (*not* Leo) Tolstoy, which had recently (1981) appeared in Slovak; the Russian edition had appeared in Leningrad in 1977. The only period work involving Leo Tolstoy's wife circulating at the time of *Kličky* ... was a Czech edition of her letters, *Sbohem, piš častěji a víc* (Farewell, write more often and more), Prague, 1981.

[93] Presumably Hrabal is referring to the then relatively recent English edition of Anna Dostoyevskaya's *Dostoevsky: Reminiscences*, New York, 1975.

down. Not that she puts me down completely; she talks about me as I am, describing all my qualities, and vices. I was driven to do it precisely by those three books I'd read, especially Mme Dostoyevsky's. Of course, I believe that Mme Pasternak's book, talking about *her* husband, has just come out somewhere in Paris,[94] but unfortunately it hasn't come my way yet. It's said to be outstanding. These women, you know... think of the Russians, they've always got a woman at their side, and the French have a woman at their side, commensurate to them. The women know who they're with and become sort of akin in spirit. My favourite painter, Jackson Pollock, who ended by getting killed in a car, had a woman at his side. Lee Krassner was her name, but she is not his Beatrice, she's the one who lived with him and was with him through all his almost metaphysical torments and always told him what he should do next, so that when she says something it's the same as if he was speaking himself. And she is still painting by gesture to this day.

Do you have a Beatrice?

No. Unfortunately. I don't have anyone to inspire me; I get my inspiration from people in pubs and people I bump into. I vaguely recall that before Polycletos of Argos started sculpting he asked the master of the Hellenic masters where to get a motif from, where he should seek inspiration. And the latter merely pointed at the people walking past them down the streets of

---

[94] This presumably refers to Olga Ivinskaya's *Otage de l'éternité. Mes années avec Pasternak*, which actually appeared in 1978 (in English in New York as *A Captive of Time. My Years with Paternak*, also in 1978).

Athens, ordinary people, and Polycletos duly made much more realistic figures because he'd trusted that act of pointing; and that's my people too, people you meet, people in the street. They are my heroes. Given I'm still here on earth, then the reason I am here is that the people I mix with, if not all of them, often give me such encouragement that I want to carry on living. Because mark this: a writer is also a person and even a writer may sometimes be in a situation where he doesn't want to go on living; everything conspires against him and there's simply too much evil in the world. He doesn't see the retreating heel, that Good might have taken a step forward, and he thinks that evil rules and he doesn't want to stay here on earth. It's those ordinary fits of the blues within us that everyone knows. What became of Mayakovsky, what came of the greatest poet in the world, Sergei Esenin – he is my greatest poet... 'Moonlit evenings, blue evenings, when I was young and all was different...' But let's change the subject. These people – suppose someone had turned up in time and knocked on the door with: 'I say, Mayakovsky, it's me, come on...', if they'd come a moment earlier Mayakovsky would still be alive. We all have such moments, like when Livy says he has never met anyone who hasn't wanted, at least once in his life, to commit suicide. And writers twice as likely. The reason a man is, or becomes, a writer is that he overcomes that profound ennui and sorrow and suddenly a spark flies up out of what looks like ash and ignites you so that you can carry on, beyond that moment when you thought you'd hit rock-bottom and were contemplating ceasing to be, but hold on! Heidegger! It's obvious from one of his treatises that 'it would be better if there were nothing', and everyone, and that means writers as well, arrives at the same point once in his life. Having overcome it and stayed alive, he takes such moments not as if he'd had his soul poisoned, but respecting them because that's where the other side is, where being arises from non-being, light from darkness, and vice versa. That is the miracle, that is that ludibrionism, those contrasting opposites, those contradictions that say that all opposites are true, so sometimes you reach the situation that you exist; and it doesn't need something to arrive from without, like being struck by lightning, as when the tarot in the Arcana Major says that you're about to lose all your property or a mistress, no, no. It's the philosophical, the poetic road that makes you suddenly see that it would be better if you didn't exist. Take Spanish philosophy. There the basis is Seneca, who committed suicide to prove what a great bloke he was, in 65 AD, somewhere in Salamanca.[95] Yet he it was who, when we read *De tranquilitate animi*, encourages others to reflect and speculate according to nature; then at a particular moment he nevertheless resolved to slit his veins open in the bath-house. Probably a bit like when Socrates drank a cup of hemlock, if for different reasons; having declined to emigrate, he said it was better to obey the laws of one's country. But that is another example, it's death, suicide, and we were talking about how a cat-lover is often forced into the situation of having to kill them. 'Whoso loves a woman, must his mistress

[95] Another of Hrabal's errors: Seneca's associations are indeed with Spain, having been born in Cordoba, but he actually died in Rome.

sometime...,' Bunin[96] wrote – God, come to the aid of my memory... 'the combined suicide of the lovers, the Tsar's cornet Yelagin and the prima ballerina of the Warsaw ballet; the young lovers, in order to be even closer, decided to depart this world together, both were dead before they died, a *unio mystica*, in order to live with greater intensity and nevermore leave each other's side...' Every such suicide or even murder has its own morality. What can be more beautiful or more justifiable than murder born of jealousy? Hasn't Shakespeare given us the evidence in Othello? He who loved, the noble savage, couldn't, by reason of his great morality, understand that his wife had lied, and so he killed her. But Heaven absolved him and he was surely received there, for he had not said 'there's more than one pebble on the beach'. No. Having played out his grand role, he achieved the communal heaven; he played out his unique purpose through which the Essence was restored. That is the essence of a good play as well: something comes from without to make things happen as they do... When Oedipus eventually tore out his eyes it was within the order of the play; all the observers who made up the second chorus knew that it had been so decreed by the gods and Oedipus was really a mere instrument... and so the æsthetic and ethical heavens were reconciled...

You are also an instrument.

Yes, I suppose I am ... I don't know how it is, but I feel... that...

[96] Ivan A. Bunin (1870–1953), Russian philosophical lyric poet and author of near-existentialist love-stories, lived abroad from 1920.

You are an instrument. Your Vladimír in Tender Barbarian *likes the urban periphery, he likes chaos. Why? And in the Foreword you hint that, in a sense, you too like chaos. And you do leave the text like a churned-up street.*

Because that's what I'm surrounded by. I live in a city, or rather on its edge. I live with people who pick things up and then just toss them down again, people who like a bit of a mess – not that they even notice it. And you get the same thing in a village. I'm much the same sort of individual, no great lover of the clean and tidy; I'm really a fairly messy, if not very messy type. The society in which I live, these Slavs who are so inclined to untidiness, are at home here, and so I'm at home here as well; it doesn't worry me. I did once tend to moralise that the reverse should be true, but it suddenly dawned that 'as you write, so the things around you look'. Hence my style: at least I get that from my environment; it's full of flaws, but that's what creates my particular charm. My lady editor tells me that when we were doing *Harlequin's Millions*[97] she received a note from the language department saying it was full of linguistic and stylistic errors, and they were all spelled out, several hundred of them.[98] But she tells them they can correct, say, fifty, but they're not to touch the rest, they give Hrabal's style its charm; they're his linguistic aberrations and we have to put up with them. If we correct them the book will lose its charm. She tells them it would be like correcting Pi-

[97] *Harlekýnovy miliony* (Prague, 1981).
[98] This refers to the circumstances, under socialism, when all publishing houses and newspaper offices etc. had a 'language department' to oversee the (linguistic) correctness of publications being prepared for printing.

casso's drawings. So if they started deleting bits, the whole thing would collapse, including the things in it that function in, so to speak, an Aristotelian, æsthetic way. So I am surrounded by mess but, honestly, I don't care, because that's the way I am. If you come to visit, if you see where and how I live, everything's there on the desk – all my writing things, medicines, all jumbled together; clothes hanging over there, slippers tossed down there. I just give the desk a wipe to give an impression of tidiness, but I don't go out of my way to keep things tidy. There's something in me that the French also have. You go to Paris, and people flick their cigarette ash everywhere; they drop their cigarette-ends and things, just like me. And it's not actually surprising, because when, under the Protectorate, I had to trace my origin, my Aryan ancestors, I found that my great-grandfather had been a French soldier who fought in the Battle of Austerlitz. He had been wounded, the local Moravian girls dragged him off and nursed him, and by the time he was fit and well Napoleon's troops were long gone and he stayed on in Moravia.

What was his name?
Kilian. French. Battle of Austerlitz, 1805.

And is your other side Czech?
Probably, though they were more likely Moravians.[99] Of course, when you look at me...

---

[99] The Moravians are also Czechs; the opposition is between Bohemian Czechs and Moravian Czechs. The problem arises from the ambiguity between *Čech* = Czech and *Čech* = Bohemian.

Mongol or Tartar...

Precisely. I always say, just look at me, one branch I come from is a mixture of Tartars, Avars, Magyars, in short I'm descended from one or other of those three; a second branch is the French one. And when we meet, it's a huge family and we always recognize one another by the broad cheek-bones. At which point you should say something about the pure Slav race. So, my liking for a degree of untidiness comes from my French origins. Whenever I go to Paris I find I've never seen such a mess, but overnight it all gets cleared up. Here I live in Prague, in a rough part, and I find it's just the same here, and that my style, with all its flaws, is exactly like the milieu I inhabit. I am a child of the times.

Doesn't it get tidied up overnight?

No. When I look at our factory yards, or our workshops, it's just like my flat. It doesn't worry me, but some kind of signalling system tells me when I cross the border, even if I'm only going to the GDR, and I can see at once the Germans have got things all neat and tidy, and their yards are fairly spruce.

What about the Hungarians?

No, not the Hungarians. That's their nature. When you cross from Moravia into Slovakia it feels like arriving in Austria – prettier houses and a fondness for flowers and vegetables; to me the Slovaks have a much higher sense of style than we do. The very fact that they observe the Sabbath, put on their Sunday best and go to church, in any village you come to, whereas Praguers? In Prague it's the foreigners who attend church. Prague people leap into their cars on Friday and half the city is depopulated. They go off to their country cottages which, remarkably enough, they do keep neat and tidy. In Prague they couldn't care less. Their homes are also tidy, but the streets and factories are a mess and I see that I'm a child of the times: I'm one of them, identical. I'd never emigrate because the pull of the environment I live in, the awful pubs I go to, is strong. None of this worries me...

Mr Hrabal, might it not be that your and our slovenliness, the pigsty mentality of our nations, is a selfish yearning for freedom?

No. I might even go so far as to say that in this country it is more a kind of protest. Most people feel they are not cut out for what they happen to be doing. Most people in this country feel they should be something else, but without knowing what. Sometimes it's a consequence of revolution. You go to the pub and any girl will start telling you she should have been something else, but she's pulling pints or working in a shop, while what she wanted was to be a doctor... And notice that: everyone here thinks they should have gone to university, they'd all like to have letters after their name. They always wish they were graduates, implying that they live in a tidy house, yet the minute they go out, they start dropping litter. And when they go to work, they heave on overalls that they wear until they fall off and mend the holes with wire! The people who go to the Harp, where I join them for lunch, deliberately go around looking like tramps, but when they go home from work, they're all washed and brushed up like me, in a fancy T-shirt and denim suit, with a neat little shoulder bag, and they walk along smugly self-absorbed. But I've been around a long time. When I lived in Nymburk and the workers turned up at the brewery on Monday, they all brought their overalls washed until they were almost pale blue, because otherwise it would have been a disgrace. At the end of a shift everything had to be tidied up and swept clean. When I lived in Židenice people also swept up, even the streets. Everyone would take a broom to the bit outside his house.

Is it also to do with our new age?

The age. Somehow people... Hell knows. It would take a psychoanalyst to explain *why* it is. *That* it is, we know; by the law of reflection we see it in *Dikobraz*,[100] and in quite horrendous pictures on the television – the stuff that people throw into once pretty streams. But why they do it, and why they used not to do it, that's a mystery. No sociologist can solve it; it's a case for psychoanalysis, not of individuals but of whole groups. Why do people sometimes have such a dreadful mess at work, yet when they go home from work each looks quite respectable? Is it protest, or indifference? I don't know.

Couldn't it be that the citizen of the new, that's to say socialist, era of this republic doesn't fully identify with the forms that constitute this society?

That brings us back to the problem of whether the society I live with, each individual, is capable, even

[100] A weekly, fairly tame satirical magazine in socialist Czechoslovakia, now defunct. Its title means 'porcupine', though its quills caused few serious pinpricks.

with no boss standing over him, of being a real husbandman. That's something President Zápotocký[101] propounded in the Fifties: 'Everyone a master in his workplace.' The principle is a noble one. We've been describing the things around us, but it also applies to me since I'm just the same, my style's the same, half-baked we might say. We live in an age of half-baked things, when you even buy half-prepared food and just finish it off at home. My own impression is that the things I write – thanks to my untidiness and lack of endurance – the things I write are half-baked. It's really my readers who have to construct them, or cook them at home, in their heads. At the age of seventy I consider myself a child of the age and a child of the environment I live in. Those days in the brewery, that was poetry, everything was beautiful, the countryside, everything; we even employed two bricklayers to maintain the fabric, so everything really was shipshape. But I moved to Libeň, now I live on this grotty urban fringe, and it's here I've written all my decent works, even though I do the actual writing in Kersko. There've been great changes at the brewery. And I've also changed.

You drew up a kind of quintet of Czech, or Prague, writers: Deml, Hašek, Klíma, Weiner and Kafka. In one way or another you have identified with each of them, but I suspect it was hardest with Kafka. Not because he's the only one who didn't write in Czech, but because you are a type of 'anti-Kafka-ist'. Perhaps that is why you mention him so often.

[101] Antonín Zápotocký (1884–1957), second Communist president of Czechoslovakia (1953–57).

I think of him because for one thing he was a doctor of laws and I too am a doctor of laws. For Kafka, literature wasn't only therapy, but a means to self-realization. You're right, of course, as regards that anti-Kafka-ist way of looking at things, since it's a question of milieu. We know that Hašek and Kafka were born in the same year and lived almost their entire lives in one and the same city. Yet they couldn't have met, because each moved in a different milieu. Kafka, as a Jew, used to go to coffee-houses and would stride across Charles Bridge with Max Brod,[102] and they would dwell on metaphysics, or sometimes Realism, but they would always be aiming – as is customary with Jews – at the metaphysical essence, symbols or ciphers. Whereas Hašek took the low road, through the pubs, so they couldn't have met, and then Kafka's narrative mode and Hašek's heroes are completely different, even though they lived in the same city. I only live in pubs. If I do end up in a coffee-house or restaurant, it's always by oversight. You'll only ever catch me dining hereabouts. I use the Harp, the Bratislava – that's a workmen's pub across the road from the Harp; it's where I pop in for lunch. So all my life I've lived where there's beer, always in workingmen's quarters, see. When I used to go to pubs in Nymburk, I always went to the ordinary small-town ones. I'm a man of the small town – a *petit bourg* – myself, but I'm not a *petit bourgeois*; that's pejorative. In Libeň you'll see the pubs where I've felt happy, and it was in just these pubs that

---

[102] Max Brod (1884–1968), Prague German-Jewish writer, living in Palestine after 1939; friend, publisher and biographer of Kafka.

Egon Bondy,[103] Vladimír – and others – and I held our debates... Obviously about art, but football as well, or uninhibited joking and swapping yarns about people. But whenever we were alone we would invariably discuss the essence of Surrealism, who Dostoyevsky really was, the basis of Existentialism; we would go over the problems facing the world or questions of literature and thought and politics, and we'd debate right here, down here. Kafka as well. Kafka... You know Kafka has matured so much that there's a new term now, kafkadom.[104] When something really stupid, some nonsense or other, crops up, Prague people call it kafkadom. Up to World War II hardly anyone knew Kafka, today he's a bestseller. Anyone reading *The Trial* or *The Castle* would have their work cut out for them to plough through all those symbols, but it took the arrival of the Wehrmacht, the annihilation of the Jews, the concentration camps, to cause the symbolic and transcendental *Castle* or *The Trial* to become simply reportage. Or a vision?

Then where do you see your kinship with Kafka?

Mine? Well take *The Trial*, which is set in Prague. The spot where Josef K. was executed – that quarry exists; the track he took, the track they led him down, it exists, and there are also books of photographs

[103] Egon Bondy, real name Zbyněk Fišer (1930–2007), Czech underground poet and philosopher, effectively banned under socialism, but widely published since 1989. He came to public notice through references to him in Hrabal's work and readings of his poetry at the Orfeus Little Theatre in Prague.

[104] The expression has previously been translated as 'Kafkorium' (W. L. Solberg), in *New Writing of East Europe*, comp. George Gömöri and Charles Newman, Chicago, 1968, pp. 179–89

which seek to reconstruct *The Trial* from particular localities. I also work from localities. Those great symbols and ciphers of Kafka's, which have ultimately proved far more realistic, more magically realist, were already there, but no one understood them. There's one particular report from *The Castle* in a stiff-backed note-book of his, and he's got a footnote on moving people to a concentration camp that dates from sometime in 1910. I bought them in Germany, those *Quartenhefte* that were never published. There you suddenly have it in one story: someone comes and knocks on the door, father gets dressed and is led away from Celetná Street,[105] never to be seen again... And the behaviour of the man who came in a leather coat – it's exactly as if Kafka had seen how the SS or the Gestapo would arrive. In other words, Kafka is part of my Prague awareness, because as Eman Frynta[106] pointed out, any crossroads where several linguistic consciousnesses meet always produces great literature. He gave Prague as an example – a Jewish-Slav-German intersection; Odessa was another, and Trieste, Zurich, crossroads where Dadaism came into being; for our own time he cites Paris, where half the artists are from Spain, Russia, Ukraine, Hungary, America, etc. He included St Petersburg, where there were also intersecting consciousnesses. I'm forever appealing to Kafka, hence I bought all those books about him. When I was in Paris it was the exact centenary of his

---

[105] A street leading off Prague's Old Town Square, part of the area associated with Kafka's life.

[106] Emanuel Frynta (1923–75), translator from Russian, author of radio 'essays' and filmscripts; wrote on Kafka and Hašek and various photographers.

birth. At a gigantic exhibition at the Pompidou Centre, where the twentieth century was pronounced as belonging to Kafka, everything was presented just as if it were taking place in Prague. A display area the size of an ice-hockey stadium to represent the Old Town Square – in a nutshell, Prague, city of a hundred spires, there in Paris... I bought all the photos and in them you can also see the area where he was inspired to write *The Castle* – it's in Frýdlant.[107] There are two books, hundreds of photos pointing to particular places where he would go and where he got his inspiration,[108] so I would go so far as to say that I've been inspired by place and reality less than Kafka was. In short, to me Kafka is a hieroglyph, just like Hašek. They are two hieroglyphs which I try to deci-

---

[107] A small town in the far north of Bohemia, close to where the Czech, German and Polish borders meet, and overlooked by an impressive castle.

[108] It is not apparent which books Hrabal is referring to here. One might well be Jiří Gruša's *Franz Kafka aus Prag* (Frankfurt a/M., 1983), also in English (trans. Eric Mosbacher) as *Franz Kafka of Prague* (London, 1983), in which the photographs are accompanied in part by Gruša's notes, in part by relevant quotations from Kafka. Gruša himself (b.1938) is a poet, translator and publisher, founder of literary journals banned in the 1960s, exiled in Germany since 1982; Hrabal would not have been able to come by the book easily, or feel free (or courageous enough) to cite an effectively banned author, which might explain why he fails to identify either book. For him to state in the next sentence that he was 'inspired by place and reality less than Kafka was' may seem slightly ingenuous, given that – besides his works in which Nymburk plays such a big part – his *toto město je ve společné péči obyvatel* (Prague, 1967), based on photographs of Prague by Miroslav Peterka, even has some points of similarity with Gruša's later work, though Hrabal's intentions are rather different (see David Short: 'Fun and games with montage: the individual case of Hrabal's *toto město je ve společné péči obyvatel*' in Short (ed.): *Bohumil Hrabal (1914–97). Papers from a Symposium* (London, 2004, pp. 59–81). Gruša's problems with the authorities came to a head with his *Dotazník aneb Modlitba za jedno město a přítele* (samizdat 1975, Toronto, 1976; in English as *The Questionnaire* [Chicago, 2000; trans. Peter Kussi]).

pher in the places where I walk, or through the legends about them. Hieroglyphs, as Mr Kroutvor[109] described them.

Hieroglyphs of the Prague consciousness?

Yes, but it's not that simple. Karel Čapek for one is much simpler, in every respect. He has his own view of things, a Neopositivist, an ace. But I am stirred by those other two, and I'll never fathom what they are, even if I buy yet more books. Radko Pytlík and I talk about it; last time it dawned on us both almost simultaneously that sometime in the future there has to come a third æstheticist and critic and artist rolled into one to try to decipher that hieroglyph; someone has to be born who will also be a psychoanalyst in order to be able to puzzle out something that is so gloriously monstrous and tender-hearted as that dead, and yet still so living writer, that Dadaist, yet Realist with it, that outstanding journalist and hoax-merchant who died at forty, just think, forty...

Kafka?

Hašek! Hašek! Jaroslav! But Kafka as well. Consider this, my friend: they were both forty and one wrote six hundred short stories and a novel which Eman Frynta has described as a pub yard overgrown into a verbal collage with the proportions of a novel...

[109] Josef Kroutvor (b. 1942), Czech art historian and critic of literature and the applied arts, who has occasionally written on Hrabal but who, in particular, appended an essay 'Central Europe: Anecdote and History' to the 1987 samizdat edition of *Pirouettes*, and gave the address on the occasion when Hrabal was awarded the George Theiner Prize at the festival of literature held during the Prague Book Fair (14 May 1992).

and the other one wrote five novels and some books of stories, and on top of that hundreds and hundreds of love-letters! And do you know what Frynta said about *The Castle*, or *The Trial*...? That they are amplified Hasidic tales! Oh, Herr Doktor Kafka! It's quite head-splitting, all those love-stories of his, all his engagements, they'll drive me insane! The moment I think about it a three-year-old cabbage grows inside my head! First engaged to Felicia Bauer, then he broke it off; then re-engaged to the selfsame Felicia; took her on honeymoon to Budapest and had his photo taken with her there. It drives me crazy! Then he broke up with her and wooed and won Milena Jesenská,[110] whose father, a university professor, had to go from Prague to fetch her because she'd been running around Vienna like Lady Godiva! And he still hadn't had enough! He broke with her and got engaged to Dora Diamant...[111] It'll be the death of me... I never got engaged even once; I've only been married once and that's quite enough for a lifetime... Ah, that Prague irony, ah, Hašek, ah, Herr Doktor Kafka... They give me hell... And do you know what else? Milena Jesenská had a daughter, Krejcarová[112] she was called, and she

---

[110] Milena Jesenská (1896–1944), Czech journalist who died at Ravensbrück; Kafka's first translator into Czech. For an introduction to Jesenská in English see Kathleen Hayes (ed. and trans.): *The Journalism of Milena Jesenská. A Critical Voice in Interwar Central Europe.* New York, Oxford, 2003, especially the editor's Introduction, pp. 1–41.

[111] Dora Diamant (1903–52), called Diamantová, also Dymantová, in Czech sources.

[112] Jana (affectionately Honza) Krejcarová (aka Jana Černá, 1928–81), daughter of Milena Jesenská and Jaromír Krejcar (1898–1949). She was something of a social and intellectual misfit who became Egon Bondy's *femme fatale*. In the late 1940s she was part of the Prague surrealist circle and in the 1950s the circle

claimed to be Kafka's daughter. She did a compilation of her mother's correspondence and wrote a novel which came out in the *Zelené osení* series; would you credit it, Mr Szigeti... But Honza Krejcarová, who became Egon Bondy's playmate and attended Karel Teige's last Surrealist seminar, is also dead now... What can you do about it?

Neither Kafka, nor Klíma had any sense of affinity with a group. Have you ever felt part of one?

When I moved to Prague I used to visit Jiří Kolář. We used to go and see him, Milan Hendrych[113] and I, because he was already a poet with several published books to his credit, and we weren't yet. We read things we'd written to him and he would comment on whether they were any good or no good, but above all he would keep us up to date about what was going on in the wider world – via Zdeněk Urbánek's[114] typewritten translations, which he would lend us. So at that time, in the Fifties, I discovered Hemingway the short-story-writer and Ring Lardner, whose short-sto-

with which Hrabal also associated (includes Bondy and Mikuláš Medek; see Note 125) and which introduced 'total realism'. Hrabal contributed an Afterword to her *Clarissa a jiné texty* (Clarissa and other texts, Prague, 1990).

[113] Milan Hendrych (1929–88), one-time director and scriptwriter for Czechoslovak Railways film studios; also wrote television plays and, being banned in the 1970s and 1980s, painted. He made Nature his central motif, along with country folk. His work raises human understanding in opposition to egoism and careerism.

[114] Zdeněk Urbánek (b. 1917), writer (novels and short stories) and translator (Joyce, Saroyan, Faulkner, Shakespeare *et al.*); proscribed between 1969 and 1989 and active in the Charter 77 movement. Latterly engaged in dramaturgy and direction at the Academy of Performing Arts, of which he was rector in 1991–92.

ries about sportsmen[115] made a great impression on me. I was the richer for these translations of short-stories. Anyway we visited him over a period of several years, believing that one day we'd also get on top of it.

And did you integrate in any group of writers later? Were you a member...

No! Never. I'm incapable of thinking *à thèse*.

And I don't think you've got many friends among writers.

No. I only meet writers when I can't avoid them, but I don't see why one writer should pal up with another anyway, unless perhaps they grew up together or made up a group with its own periodical. And we didn't.

And not even now?

No. And that's probably a good thing...

And do you read the manuscripts of young writers, like Jiří Kolář read yours?

No. If they do give me any, I send them back very quickly saying I haven't got time, or that... anyway I don't read them.

---

[115] Ring Lardner (1885–1933), American journalist, short-story writer and satirist, who displayed the stupidity and ineptitude of his 'ordinary' characters with wit and some pessimism. He became popular with a wide general readership well before he was noticed by the critics. The 'short-stories about sportsmen' are letters by 'Jack Keefe', an imaginary newcomer to a baseball team, which Lardner published in the *Chicago Tribune* (1916). In 1910–11 he had edited a St Louis baseball weekly and was a sports reporter for various US papers.

So you're not one for editing or mentoring?

No. I'm not the editing type and my eyes hurt. My eyes hurt, so I'd rather they tell me orally. When I finish my own things, my eyes are so exhausted that it's hard to read. I read little enough as it is, so I'm not going to read a hundred and fifty pages for somebody else – and then write a commentary to boot. Sometimes, when I get a conscience, I do write the odd review...

Part of my reason for asking whether you belonged to any group of writers was that in the beat generation several groups were born.

Yes. A Kerouac or a Ginsberg couldn't fail to fertilize my age-group. I'm fascinated by Kerouac and Ginsberg, and by Ferlinghetti, indeed by all those who followed in the wake of the 'dharma bums', who had an acute sense that a writer should be poor for as long as possible, simple for as long as possible, and at rock-bottom for as long as possible, so that he can gaze upwards. And he should be educated, and he should enjoy – and this goes without saying – oriental wisdoms. We've spoken about Zen buddhism, we've mentioned the Upanishads,[116] we've mentioned Lao Tzu; the boys I'm talking about, that group of beatniks, those dharma bums, they knew all of that. Some visited Tibet; it wouldn't particularly matter that they went there, what does matter is that they derived prac-

---

[116] This is probably an instance where Hrabal's method of cutting and pasting, to which he repeatedly refers and which applies to the present book as well (as explained in some detail in 'PS 1' in the original), has let him down; any reference to the Upanishads as such herein is lost, though there are recurrent references to 'Indian philosophy', which he doubtless has in mind at this point.

tical consequences from it, and they were who they were. At a distance I was in a group with them

But they didn't just kick up a noise; they also knew how to write.

No doubt about that. Everything that appeared in *World Literature*[117] or came out as books – Kerouac in *Railroad Earth* and his *On the Road* – to me it's all literature written by a young man. And you could describe, say, *Fire Watcher*, one of Kerouac's short-stories, as beautiful beyond words, one of the most beautiful short-stories ever written, breathtaking. Ginsberg came to Prague. I spoke to him at Hanzlberk – an abandoned house taken over by a group of young people sometime in 1965, which became a squat for painters and poets and the dancers Turba[118] and Boris Hybner,[119] and the photographer 'Ahasver',[120] and Ginsberg was their guest. I suspect it was in 1968, when there was a Spring festival in Prague; at a kind of student procession or May Fest they carried Ginsberg in white trainers on a float and declared him Festival King. He was bearded and kept bowing, and next day I caught up with him at Hanzlberk, where he was the

[117] *Světová literatura*, a solid literary journal that published translations of recent works of foreign literature. In the 1990s it became an irregular miscellany and ceased publication in 1994.
[118] Ctibor Turba (b. 1944), actor, puppeteer, author and director, now working in the Department of Non-Verbal Art of a Performing Arts Academy; previously in the Dance Department of a Faculty of Music.
[119] Boris Hybner (Czechicised form of his real name Hübner) (b. 1941), Czech mime and actor, scriptwriter and director; founder (1976), later leader, of the *Gag* group and of the 1990 Studio Gag.
[120] Pseudonym of Pavel Hudec (b. 1941), a major Czech art photographer, widely published and exhibited. His Studio Ahasver publishing house produces post-cards, calendars and posters.

guest of Boris Hybner and Turba and 'Ahasver', the photographer, and the several dozen others who lived there. The beatniks – that was a generation that electrified me as well; you could say the whole of young Prague was set alight by them. Suddenly, here was a group that lived what it proclaimed. A group of bums, hipster angels, as they also called themselves, who risked their lives, and they had their hero, Moriarty, a character who I don't know whether he exists, but he existed. Kerouac is dead. Moriarty is there though, and so many people projected themselves into him; he's one of the main characters threading through *On the Road* as well. He's forever crossing the entire continent, from San Francisco to New York and back and in a permanent state of euphoria, in permanent ecstasy.

Since you were so fascinated by their ideas, would you mind telling me what the basic point was?

I believed what I read – that it was something that was also lived. That there was no difference between the poet's life and the character written about; that they were identical. So I believed them. There was always something religious about it; life is a kind of fascination which always tends, at the very least, to the transcendental. What goes beyond reality is the driving force on the horizon, it's the road, life as such. It all follows on from Lao Tzu, the philosopher Lao Tzu and his book of Tao, and Tao is the road. But the Lao Tzu that wrote it is an old man, while Kerouac wrote *On the Road* as a young man. Above all I admired the way he always wrote in a steady stream. A stream of thought. *On the Road* was written in a very short space of time. Like a blacksmith's bellows, in, out.

What did you and Ginsberg talk about?

I don't know any English and I vaguely recall that he didn't talk much to anybody. He just kept bowing and he didn't have an interpreter. We didn't need to communicate. Dogs don't either. He bowed to me, I bowed to him, he bowed to everybody, people drank, there was music, somebody playing the guitar. So it was rather like a rowdy pub where you can't talk, where can't make yourself heard above the hubbub. It was always terrifically noisy, and then Boris Hybner, one of the best male dancers in Europe, as he is even now – look how he danced yesterday in Prague, a European prodigy is Boris Hybner – and Turba, he's lecturing somewhere in Switzerland, but in those days, when Ginsberg was here, they danced and did their thing at Hanzlberk, and that's why Ginsberg felt at home here with these madmen of his. At Hanzlberk he felt an absolute identity and absolutely at home. *Omnia ubique.*

And what about Forman? One Flew over the Cuckoo's Nest?

Yes, I saw the film. By accident. I haven't read the book. I'd been to have a look at the Hockenheim racetrack; nowadays it's for motor racing and they even hold the European championships there, but in the past it was motor-cycle championships. When I went to have a look at the circuit I spotted an advert for *Einer flog über Kuckucksnest*. So that evening I went to see it. The odd thing was that the audience consisted almost entirely of young people, and they laughed and laughed at it; I didn't find it at all funny. They were looking for an excuse to laugh. Rather stupid young people. You can be sure that if it had been in, say, Heidelberg, in the city – and Heidelberg is a university town – it would have been properly appreciated. But this was outside the city, so it was a sort of confusing environment. I was deeply affected by the film, especially the lead, that madman. The one who on the other hand isn't quite mad, but so what if he is – he wants freedom for his fellow-madmen and wins it for them by finding at least one moment when they can have a fling on the boat. I say nothing of the head nurse, that giant figure, that vehicle of power, or of the moral justification for intervening when it seems... but the film and its ending... actually McMurphy only had one disciple, and that's the Red Indian, who, after going to pieces, yanks the safe or whatever off the wall and uses it to smash through the wall. So the film is fully on the side of the 'insulted and injured' madmen, and, incidentally, there's a superb actor plays in it, I can't remember his name, or, yes, Jack Nicholson! Well, this man Nicholson, what a superb actor, but Forman's directing was also superb – the way he handled his source material. The art of reducing it to an hour and a half – that's the secret of Forman's genius. That film had a message for the entire world and could be shown in any city anywhere in the world. And it didn't even have to have sound; it could be a silent film and people would still understand it. That's where I see its greatness. Almost like the age of the old silent films. There's still some mileage in old things...

What other experiences do you retain from the art of the beat age?
None. What I had was sufficient. I can make do with *Fire Watcher* and the æsthetics that appeared somewhere in 1966–67 in *World Literature*. The readers were treated to about forty pages of information on the beatniks, and that was enough for me. I can make do with a photograph showing what Kerouac was like. I can always get by with photos. Ginsberg I saw in the flesh, I read several of his poems, and I simply believed him. Of course I never expected him to die so relatively young. But here, the beat community was Hanzlberk. At Hanzlberk people lived as the beatniks lived. Where I lived in Libeň, in the Fifties, people also lived like that. Vladimír Boudník was there, Egon Bondy; Medek[121] would come, and Zbyněk Sekal,[122] the Suprasectdadaists[123] were there, Jelínek.[124] We could pirouette off in a new direction in a space the size of a postage stamp...

At No. 24, Na hrázi?
Yes, there in that room. Where the sun couldn't reach...

[121] Mikuláš Medek (1926–74), Czech surrealist, existentialist and abstract painter and poet.
[122] Zbyněk Sekal (1923–98), Czech painter and sculptor, living abroad since 1970; inspired by the Surrealists, but as a sculptor he was a leader in structural abstraction.
[123] See Note 125.
[124] Oldřich Jelínek, Czech graphic artist, illustrator, painter and caricaturist (b. 1930 in Košice, Slovakia).

In your flat?

Of course. They lived there a year or two, and even longer. They had their groups – the Surrealists, Total Realists, Suprasexdadaists[125] – those were the Fifties. So what you had in America, I reckon came earlier in Prague... And I'm sure it was the same in Budapest or Cracow, or Vienna, but there wasn't the publicity – what the Americans are so good at in order to make things happen. All they needed was to have their own programme, a conception, and their own publisher, like Ferlinghetti. And five years was plenty, then the community could perhaps break up; but five years were enough for them to live together, form connections, and give the thing a style. It's just the same as the reaction against the cultural and social conditions in the US, where those young people took matters into their own hands and expressed those conditions exactly. Enough of consumer society, enough of those intellectuals, enough enlightened and enlightening lecturing, that crap. Action, get up and do. Theorising and philosophising are an integral part of it all; it's simply a reaction – as we might put it – to the total identity of two opposites. Spirit and life. With the beatniks it was like the Koh-i-Noor 'Waldes' patent press-stud. In that they had an identity.

[125] This is the name adopted by one of the post-Avant-garde groups in Prague. Both the 1987 and 1990 editions of this work preserve, as in the MS, the misquotation of the name at the first occurrence (previous page), while the Collected Works edition uses the correct -*sex*- form for both. The editors of the latter note: '...the author, at the Golden Tiger restaurant on 12 December 1995, pronounced the error "superb".' It is worth mentioning here that in his later years Hrabal regularly 'held court' at the Golden Tiger, which accordingly became a place of pilgrimage for his numerous fans.

They were most interested in issues of sex and meditation, and at the same time they would talk about not wanting anything to do with America, but loving America none the less.

But of course. That America – it's Whitman's America. The America of the beatniks goes on in the spirit of Whitman, tending towards realistic mysticism... The mystical method.

Sex, meditation and the degradation of power.

Sandburg was another of their spiritual fathers. Carl August Sandburg, the chap who really earned his living playing the guitar. Look, they didn't mince their words when they talked about politics and power. They called a spade a spade. I live in a country where, as a loyal citizen, I have to be polite and proper to my political representatives, and render what is Caesar's to Caesar and what is existential – to me. So I do play the role of citizen, but on top of that the role of a super-citizen because I feel that I'm also one of those children of God. A man who has the finger-print of something bigger, something that is more than the state, more than even the Party. I don't think that goes against the spirit of those people of mine who I've loved – Seryozha Esenin and the others, say. I'm a little Socrates, except for the hemlock.

When you started writing poems, did you know Ezra Pound? Had anything of his appeared in Czech?

World literature again. I believe Ezra Pound *was* also published in it. He's another of those phenomena that fascinate. He's also a poet with that finger-print. A real writer, a proper penman! The timeless trickled into his time...

But then his playfulness...

That's the essence of being a poet. The essence of a poet is play. Male play, honest-to-goodness play. The child that matures inside a boy or a man is brought to a kind of perfection by the poet. Nietzsche has that whole glorious chapter on the subject. About the child playing inside the man. He describes it as a wheel that starts turning on its own, and only as a mature adult can you achieve what you'd dreamed of as a child. And as a child you would dream legends and various deceptions which are so very like poetic creation and contain the kind of thing that even the seemingly highly realistic Fellini alludes to; in essence though, Fellini is also a great Romantic who prefers fictions to the truth. And what is fiction?

Fiction is play.

An *idée fixe*, or the *grand jeu*. Even in *8 ½* you can tell he was playing at directing, playing in the Ladislav Klíma sense. That divine game, that fiddly, crazy and yet stupid game, ludibrionism. Fellini was playing games even in *8 ½*. He made it without knowing what was going to come next and he got enormously excited by it. Or he pretended not to know what he was going to do next. This was his demonstration of the creative individual's *Angst*. But the creative individual is also like that child, he enjoys going back to his childhood. So in *8 ½* even his late parents appear, and little Fellini himself is there, then later he made the entire film *Amarcord* about his childhood and boyhood. Boyhood really... Let's leave Ezra Pound out, since he's not someone I'd read every year, unlike Whitman. Do you know why? I haven't got him at home. I only ever read what I can lay my hands on or what people give me.

You began as a poet, and do you know what Faulkner maintained? Maybe every novelist would first like to write poetry. And as I read your latest novel, Loud Solitude, *it's one monumental poem.*[126]

It was organic. I wrote poems from – let's say 1936, and I stopped in the 'Fifties.

But you're still writing poems. Too Loud A Solitude,[127] *for me it's a truly monumental poem.*

A ballad; and a ballad does have a particular aura...

Talking of ballads brings us back to Faulkner. He's one for mystification, yet his colours are much darker than yours.

He's American, a Southerner; I'm a man of *Mittel-Europa*. But you're quite right to mention Faulkner. For a long time he was, for me, not exactly alien; I've read several of his earlier novels, but the stories about Negroes, they cut deep into me, they're like ground glass – it's as if instead of reading you're eating ground glass. Only in the last ten years or so... my *Dancing Lessons for Older and Intermediate Learners*,[128] it's a stream of narration which ought to be analogous to Molly Bloom's, that's to say Joyce's. But the endless sentences, those long, long sentences of Faulkner's, those

[126] The first variant of *Hlučná samota* was indeed in verse.

[127] *Příliš hlučná samota*, 1977, 1978, 1979, 1986 in samizdat editions, 1980 (Cologne), 1989 first regularly published edition in Czechoslovakia. Given the time of the interview, Szigeti may be referring to one of the 'illegal' editions of this book, though it had also appeared in translation in Hungary.

[128] *Taneční hodiny pro starší a pokročilé*, 1964 (and numerous later editions, also in Hungarian translation since 1971), a work without punctuation.

ribbons... In recent years I've felt an affinity with Faulkner in sensing a need for such endless sentences. I'd hardly go any further than inserting commas and just the odd full-stop. With him I expect it was the same as what I feel myself, just breathing in and breathing out. I inhale images and then exhale them over a period. Like when a smoker takes a drag and then savours the smoke from it much longer. That's been the rhythm of my writing in recent years and subsequently I've discovered that that was probably how Faulkner wrote his main novels, too. This inhaling and exhaling, what's called the cosmic breathing of things, the rhythm that's like – as Lao Tzu puts it in *The Canonical Book of Virtues* – a smith's bellows, and it always has to have you ready for writing, as an athlete's got to be prepared in order to jump two metres thirty. It needs a huge accumulation of images, great concentration, or patient waiting for the time to be ripe, by when the particular issues and sentences are already installed in me, and then it can start gushing and pumping like the bellows. Like when you feel the smoke, the inhaling and exhaling, simply that cosmic rhythm which you also transfer over the years to your writing. Surprisingly, when he was writing, Kerouac had it too. In *On the Road* he writes that to avoid having to keep putting paper in his typewriter he got hold of paper in rolls, put one roll in the typewriter and typed a hundred metres at a time. Here you can see how playful it is, this rhythm of breathing, this accumulation so that no image is let slip. The trilogy[129] I'm

[129] See Note 88, 90.

currently writing, the narrative by my wife, is simply written *alla prima*.

Which part are you on?
I'm sort of revising part two. I might...

And you're writing the third.
Beginning it. It could...

Faulkner, Joyce and Musil[130] *and all other authors of great novels have pondered the novel's future. István Örkény has said that the reason he writes short novels is that nowadays people don't have so much time for reading as in the past.*

And I would agree. But as you can see: the novel has got the green light. Take the one that has had Prague spellbound: *Sophie's Choice*. Here's an American, another Southerner, who's written a six-hundred-page novel and taken Prague's breath away. A hard-hitting novel dealing with a profound problem, written by an American about Europe, Nazi Europe, the Europe of Poles living in Cracow and Warsaw during the war. It's all narrated through Sophie, and yet it takes place in Brooklyn. It's rhythm at play, again it's sort of picking up on Joyce and Céline,[131] or Henry Miller. In other words this Southerner is very well informed, he knows how to get things down, and he has structure... The guy's name's Styron.

---

[130] Robert Musil (1880–1942), Austrian novelist and a major innovator in the German-language novel; his work gives a critical analysis of modern European society.
[131] Louis-Ferdinand Céline (1894–1961), French author of stories criticising French bourgeois society, written largely in slang.

So you think the novel has got the green light. Which reminds me of Henri Matisse, who said that the older a man gets, the quicker he wants to say what he has to say. He was about seventy, roughly like you now, when he said: 'I think I've learned enough from painting to be able to move on to grand compositions.' So what about your trilogy?

I can't give you a report on that because it's not ready yet, though part one could be, and maybe part two... the third still lies ahead... What I can say is that part one is written in the manner of the classical short-story or novella; part two is written as a stream without punctuation... and part three? I'm still hesitating... I tell myself that if Goethe could write a novel in letters, why couldn't I write a novel as a long interview... But we'll see: the thing is, a writer should only exhibit what he's already written, and at most he should derive from what he's written his writing method and style... Otherwise he ought to keep things a bit secret, because if I told you what I want to write it would cost me my secret. I think we've already said plenty... and in truth, sometimes the less said the better... Anyway, these answers are draining my blood, as if you were eating my brain away with a tea-spoon... I'm actually pretty cryptogamous, you know...

Mr Hrabal, you like playing games; me too. As a way of refreshment, let's try the following game: What do you think of if I utter the word 'hell'?

Life. Orphan.

Why?

Do you mean to say such hell can't exist? It's as

Hieronymus Bosch portrayed it for us, as he painted it... The orphaned child...

Touches.
Fingers. The rhombus of Michaelis.[132]

Why that in particular?
I'm a tactile sort of chap, I have to touch things all over, simply... I don't know why! Three gorgeous dimples on a young woman's back...

A noise.
Hardly anything... More like silence, so... Silence... You can only hear sounds against a background of silence... If there were no silence, there'd be no noise. There has to be silence for there to be sound. Silence.

What springs to mind if I say 'failure'?
Me.

Why? After all, you're a celebrated writer. Aren't you satisfied?
I don't consider myself a... I've always been more driven by others, I... except for odd moments I've no reason for thinking I'm happy, or that I... Failure – you

---

[132] Gustav Adolf Michaelis (1798–1848), German obstetrician, whose classic work *Das enge Becken nach eigenen Beobachtungen und Untersuchungen* (posth., Leipzig, 1851) continues to be widely cited; this reference is omitted from the index of names in Hrabal's collected works; that index is admittedly only a 'selection' and lists 'persons who are generally well known, verifiable or connected with [Hrabal]' (Miroslav Červenka *et al.*, *Sebrané spisy Bohumila Hrabala. Sv. 19. Bibliografie, Dodatky, Rejstříky*, Prague, 1997, p. 113). The omission of Michaelis is slightly surprising given that the association between the rhombus and 'touches', as arising in this bout of free association is by no means 'free', as various manuals of midwifery will confirm.

see I love ruination, I love hangovers. If I've ever had a noble thought, then it's always been at a moment like that, with a hangover, or shortly afterwards. Meaning a condition of being at rock-bottom and gazing upwards...

Blood.

Pain. A red line across a white wall...

Love.

Pain... Torment... that's better, torment. Love, torment... for two.

Friendship.

Light. Tiny slivers of eternity... the church.

Compassion.

Faintness. A lost river.

Water.

Cold... and unpleasantness... A return ticket.

Warmth.

Red, red of course!

Where did you get red from?

Well, it can't be blue. Warmth, red. It's pretty general. Blood is warm, the colour of banners.

Let's imagine I'm fifteen or sixteen and I ask you to advise me how to live.

It's my firm belief, and I know from my own life – when I was that age, I was acutely aware of a sort of private, inner home tutor inside me who would tell me, advise me, spontaneously, what to do. Whenever I did it, I know it was always disastrous. And those disasters, whether with a pretty girl or friends, meant I had to overcome something. It always began with the first thing my inside advised me to do after I asked myself; my private tutor. Whenever I tried to make up my mind what to do, my spontaneous private tutor would tell me. So I would set off down the path indicated. I looked neither left nor right and felt as if the road ahead was being laid out before me and guarded behind me by angels. Now I come to think of it, there is a certain hero, but it could actually be anyone, described by the author of *The Metaphysics of Tragedy* – once a Hegelian, ultimately a Marxist, one of the best æstheticists of Europe, or the world I think, and that's...

Lukács?[133]

Of course! He's another one of *my* authors. Another of my teachers. Without him I'd be standing here like a gate half-hanging off its hinges...

Yes, but that was the young Lukács. And did that spontaneity, your private tutor, really always tell what to do and how to do it?

Reason certainly didn't. Remember that Dostoyevsky tells us that people would never get far on reason alone. I've never asked anyone, because whenever I did I was absolutely invariably impelled to do the opposite. Even as a child I was awkward, an awkward so-and-so... Poor mother.

[133] György Lukács (1885–1971), Hungarian philosopher and æstheticist, theorist of the novel and modern drama.

I expect you've had loves and friends who have disappointed and left you.

Of course. My angels have disappeared. Then I had to probe with my feet to find I was almost on the edge of the precipice. Like a true trapper I'd say I had to wait. I did wait. I waited anxiously, in a real darkness, and I would wait for a light somewhere, a hint, someone almost to give me a hand, one of my friends, or I would hear that voice we were talking about. If someone had knocked at Mayakovsky's door at that critical juncture, he wouldn't have blown his brains out. It just needed that moment to be overcome, but no one came, neither friend, nor wife, in short in Mayakovsky's case it must have been like me, he was simply waiting... I would wait for weeks in a state of anxiety, sweating, gaunt, bleary-eyed, until someone came from outside, and it was actually that angel in disguise; Uncle Pepin came, an angel disguised as Uncle Pepin, as Karel Marysko,[134] or as... Olinka Micková[135] came and said: 'Bogan, come on, let's go for a game of tennis'... But I've never been in such a predicament that I might have jumped under a train or drowned myself, on the contrary.

And what about death, Mr Hrabal?

I've sent death packing once already. You know, death is a letter written in white chalk on a white board, death is a jammed typewriter, a self-acting ma-

---

[134] Karel Marysko (1915–1988), one of Hrabal's closest lifelong friends, a cellist with the orchestra of the National Theatre in Prague. The text of *Jarmilka* was found in his locker. I am indebted to Radko Pytlík for this information.

[135] Olina Micková (??-??, but see note 88). Pytlík believes she was one of Hrabal's girlfriends from Nymburk.

chine churning out random rejects, a menacing, invisible hand without fingers, death is an express train falling into a bottomless chasm, the scattered bodies from a plane that has exploded. But right up to the last there is hope of life. Fears that there's nothing to be afraid of anymore. This very evening you'll be sharing your dinner-table with Abraham. But God knows I'd rather not eat. I've sent death packing... by wanting to live.

You have already said that after the accident you saw people differently. Were you close to death?

Ever since my operation I've seen people differently. I can tell from a distance who's nursing his gall-bladder, which dodderer is diabetic; I see his harried eye, that sweet sickness you have to attack with bathroom scales and your watch in your hand; I can recognise a damaged liver from ashen features, I can tell who's going to kick the bucket within six months, those eyes that are constantly saying good-bye to things, already looking round the other side of the door-handle. I can see most people limping and tottering, I can see the tics in sleepless eyes, I can spot a hand pressed against a thyroid, I can see the wrinkles caused by the extraction of canines, I can see the cautious chewing action of dentures and paradentosis; I see the painful gait of calcarate heels, the shaking fingers of chronic drinkers; I see women in tears coming out of hospitals where they've left their husbands, I see men leaving funeral parlours where they've just booked their wives' funerals; and I see the only fit ones, young people who are happy not to be afflicted by their glands or by love. How come I hadn't seen this before? Or that I'd not seen things properly? The reason there are so few suicides is that when your breathing's all buggered up you start hoping and believing that the cancerous ulcer will disappear, that your cancer-ridden lungs will be cured by radiation, that a miracle will happen, you see; that's why you get those beautiful leave-taking eyes which are forever saying good-bye to someone. You know, of all instruments my favourite is the needle. Instead of a head it has a little eye through which the thread is passed, and only then can you start sewing. There are times when I gaze up into the moonlit sky and get an acute sensation that someone up there is threading the moonlight into my brain, and so I discover things I knew nothing about. I suspect that the greatest misfortune that could befall humanity is excessively healthy people. So the healthiest people in the world are sick and full of suffering... Insulted and injured.

Have you ever contemplated suicide?

In literary terms all the time. In literature I'd be on the point of... But to get up and head for the water, never. I've preferred to remain in desperation, profound melancholy. I never even asked my parents what to do, because I knew I'd get advice that was too sensible and too inappropriate to my predicament. I knew I was too young, too silly-naive, in other words I was that solid bell of ignorance that must apply to any young person, and afterwards, as you can see, I always took off. I loved football, I was even good at the game, and I've got fractures acquired playing. One of the high-spots for me is a Hidegkuti[136] pirouette on a postage stamp; it's like how to switch metaphors. *The Fascination*.[137]

Did you ever see him play?

Of course! Hidegkuti's pirouette on a postage stamp that can turn a game around.

And where did you see him?

First the Hungarians thrashed us five-one, then in Prague we beat them five-three. I saw that game. But I've also read about the match of the century, when the Hungarians won six-three in England.[138] And seven-two in Budapest.[139] Sapper Vodička[140] would have had a heart attack!...

And who do you support now?

Scotland and England.

---

[136] Nándor Hidegkuti (1922–2002), the deep-lying centre-forward in Hungary's 'golden' national football team of the 1950s. For four years the 'Mighty Magyars', built around goalkeeper Gyula Grosics (b. 1926), right-half József Bozsik (1925–78) and the inside-forwards Sándor Kocsis (1929–79), Hidegkuti and Ferenc (Fero) Puskás (b. 1927), were unbeatable.

[137] In English in the original.

[138] This was at Wembley in 1952, and terminated England's reputation for invincibility; it followed on the heels of Hungary's capture of the Olympic title in that year. England's further crushing by the Hungarians in Budapest came the following year.

[139] Sources put this score at 7–1.

[140] Sapper Vodička is the strong-armed swaggerer in Jaroslav Hašek's *Adventures of the Good Soldier Schweik*, who is so virulently anti-Hungarian that even Schweik is frequently dismayed, as in the exchange: "'Hungarians are, in a word, scum.' But Schweik countered: 'Some Hungarians can't really help being Hungarian though.'"

So that explains the Union Jack spread across your bed?

Look here, when they broadcast a match from over there you get football as it should be, and a crowd as it should be. And even if the fans start fighting, it's the right backdrop for decent football to be played against. I reckon they actually play to that backdrop and the backdrop helps them on. I reckon England could muster five national teams, while we've got our work cut out to raise one.

But we've digressed: do you know what problems young people have?

Hm, their problems are actually mine too: whether Slavia will win, or Sparta, or Bohemians,[141] what suit to buy; I just sit around with them in pubs, they come up to me, I autograph beer-mats for them, we chat, then they ask about this or that – every day I spend some time with them in the pub. And I think that's great, but the last ten years I've done more listening to them talking and observing the relations among them, or I also sit up and take note wherever I see a pretty girl or a handsome lad.

And what are their relations? How do you see them?

I dunno. Either they like each other, or they don't.

Are there a lot of divorces?

There must be. Everyone I talk to is divorced. I don't know why that should be. I don't know what sport there is in it; and I don't know how it is in Buda-

---

[141] This reference is to the three main Prague football teams.

pest either – that's also Middle Europe. But I even read an article in *Rudé právo*[142] the other day that said that every third marriage in Prague breaks down. Then it's the children that suffer, and the pets...

What do you think is behind it?

No idea. I don't know why people get divorced. They're too touchy, touchy, don't you think? They're all worried about their bloody honour, and if you've too much bloody honour, it's a load of shit, as we say in Czech, because that's when marriage breaks down. One partner must be submissive, indulgent, then it will work. If both are temperamental, both insist on being right, then the marriage can't fail to break down. And come to that, why on earth can't people wait to... I got married when I was forty-two. The people I'm talking about usually get married even before their military service or straight after it, and in this country they've already got a family at twenty-one, and at twenty-five, when they've had two children, they dash out with their club banner shouting 'Long live Sparta!' and hare off to the pub with the lads. But I make no judgements – it's just what I see, what I've registered – because I haven't got divorced; it's never even occurred to me. At most I've thought I could wring my wife's neck, but any bloke worth his salt sometimes gets the urge to wring his wife's neck, and vice versa – the wife would be glad if her better half, her treasure, were run over by a bus... No, it would never occur to me to consider divorce; would there be anything to gain from it? I think

---

[142] *Rudé právo*, the Czechoslovak Communist Party daily.

not. So I just look at them as if they were confused little children; adults starting on about divorce strike me as like retarded children. Or as adults, but starting to suffer convulsions, like butchers with gout. It's all some sort of period trend. When I was young, I remember there was always this engagement thing. Girls got engaged, once, twice, and only got married the third time. But today, engagement has become marriage, since people are cheerfully married three times – every tenth person you meet. And they're quite jolly, happy about it, not having breakdowns, so it's a social trend that goes with the age we live in. Let's take it further: today's young people sort of live only ten years, then it's anyone's guess what comes next. But my generation lived much longer ahead, twenty years or so. People did marry, but only after going out together for four years; there was love at first sight, but marriage only came later. When they'd got a few things together they would marry. That's why I like those women who stay by their man, like certain birds or animals. There are many monogamous birds and animals who stay together. There was a swan at Nymburk, and when she died the cob flew straight at a bridge-pillar and killed himself; committed suicide. Or the stork: when a stork gets hurt and can't fly, his lady will stay on the ground with him and even freeze to death with him – she can't help herself. So I don't know why humans shouldn't stay together. And the misery... You'll always have misery, there are always things to make you miserable, like the disparity between ideals and reality – how things are and how they ought to be. You see, when engaged couples live apart, they can only meet and talk when they get dressed up for it and prepare for it as a routine, as it were. Whereas when you marry, you sleep in the same bed, wash in the same bathroom, use the same toilet, you keep bumping into each other, and then things go to pot. The shared programme starts to crumble and it's never quite as you'd imagined it. But let's stop talking about it – these are problems I'd rather avoid… The ideal and spleen… shock…

So I've noticed, which is why I asked. But you are married.

Yes, and happily. Despite the fact that when I want something and ask my wife's advice she wants the opposite. Okay, I say; I play it psychologically and in order to get my way, I say and make out that I want what I really don't want. But my wife can read me and suddenly agrees with me, thereby achieving what she had wanted and what I hadn't. Idiots are much better off, but if you try something on with a university-educated woman, you're bound to lose. So society is slowly but surely moving towards matriarchy, and four years with no school certs is better than a classical education. And Hidegkuti's pirouettes on a postage stamp on top of that…

You take a pretty dim view of…

Dim view indeed! What kind of view do you expect me to have when my two sworn enemies have been my mother and my wife? The one handed me over to the other and they've both been committed to my constant upbringing and improvement. So I keep fleeing from home and taking up residence in even the scruffiest pub, where I'm on tenterhooks in case the door opens and my wife walks in with my late mother as superstructure. I've been so much in the safekeeping of two much-loved women that we've become mortal enemies and sclerosis has set in. So my only option has been to seek salvation in writing and through literature cleanse myself of all that those two well-intentioned good souls had instilled in my slightly discordant soul. I never found the strength to cut up the common bed-sheet and go off in the night, because weakness is my strength, defeat my victory; the ideas that come on the steps outside are the real ideas I forgot to mention in court; being scared witless is my heroism; being alone is my being peopled; my maundering is my rhetoric; the folklore of the city is my æsthetics; permanent abandon is my punctuality; failing to keep my word is my loyalty. So all failings and vices are the needle of my compass, always pointing to a virtuous and beautiful Pole Star, that silent and motionless star around which all else revolves. In the sky every yes has its no, but one milligram of prevailing good sets everything in motion, only for it to stand stock still again through the eternal process of return, but only for one tiny, teeny-weeny moment until it starts all over again. That's my collection of samples which I'd never claim have no commercial value...

And what does your wife have to say about it?
My wife looks on me as a stupid child, and it's only now that I'm writing the book where my wife tells the story of our marriage. It's that trilogy.[143] Or rather, it's

[143] See note 90.

more an excuse for story-telling. I've already written the story of my parents' marriage – they stayed together all the way to the old people's home. They never contemplated divorce, and yet young people today...

What's your message for young people?

Every young person should find the plank along which he, and he alone, should walk. Every young person has his genius, each one is surrounded by a solid bell of ignorance; the most beautiful thing about a young person is a kind of defiant self-assurance, but also the sense that he is not alone in the world, that there are others besides him, that he is part of a human society. Not any society, but one which is seeking a better world even at the price that the young person is the only one still defending the essence and contours of that glorious idea... And the same thing should apply in marriage...

Mr Hrabal, when did you write Too Loud a Solitude?

It must have been in 1974. If I have produced any mature work, then that is the peak of my maturity. In my own way, I wasn't trying to write anything more than that one era was coming to an end and another approaching. The hero Hanťa, who was used to doing everything in the old way, by hand, embodies a breaking-point in Czech society, with machinery arriving on the scene. It was meant to be realistic, yet it's also symbolic. That whole age had lasted for several hundred or a thousand years, and Hanťa is at the break; the splinters of the plank are in him. Hanťa was a living person, but he lacked the intellectual charge which I give him. So he's real; we were both drunkards. What's expressed in that noisy solitude is the point at which one era has reached breaking-point and another, new one, is beginning, which, as you know, doesn't happen all that often in human society. It only ever happens once. Long ago the age of Classical antiquity came to an end and the Christian era began. A completely new way of thinking. The ones who suffered then were those who lived in the old, classical ways because they couldn't imagine anything else. And then a completely new model came along again, a model not only of thinking, not only of philosophical understanding, but of a way of life and of the structure of society. And your Mr Hrabal's job was to record the change. I recorded it in such a way that it can be read like Hašek's *Schweik*. Though compared to Hašek it's a bit more like quality literature. But nowadays the Czech reader, your arithmetically average Czech reader, is more sophisticated. My method, which here and there rises to poetry, does not create the problem for the reader of failing to draw him into the content. A book of mine can always be read twice over. Either just as it is, or taking account of what its symbolic meaning might be. Except that I usually don't want there to be any symbolism. For me it's all real.

But you don't always manage.

People go and put the symbols in *ex post*. What it might mean, trying to expound what they take as allegory. No. *A priori*, I never want to write either in symbols or allegory. But if on the off-chance – then it's a Hidegkuti pirouette on a postage stamp...

But the reader is creative and takes your ideas further. After all, you said yourself that your novels are like half-ready meals.

Yes, I did. Anyone can spice them up with their own imaginings...

Are they your memoirs?

No, I wouldn't say that, not memoirs. More like an experience that keeps following me around until it matures sufficiently for the right moment to arrive – the way it is for a woman before childbirth – for me to see things quite clearly and precisely and do little more than copy it out. For it to keep growing as I write, but there has to be the right moment, the right degree of ripeness. I also wrote *Closely Observed Trains*; I spent ten or a dozen years working on that in my head too. There's no way of speeding things up. Quite suddenly you sense you haven't got just the content, but that the content then determines the form for you.

So what you're saying is that you need to distance yourself from the event.

Of course. I wrote *Too Loud a Solitude* in 1973 or 1974, but I'd got the factual side together in the recycling centre, living it to the full from 1954 to 1958. But the experience of those four years was so compelling that it couldn't recede as the years progressed; on the contrary, it kept being topped up, filled out. You must understand, it was topped up by what was laid over it, or even by fictitious elements, things that hadn't happened, or had happened elsewhere, or things I was told by someone else, but which sat perfectly with my obsession. Then only when it had matured, when it made a whole inside, was I able to sit down and write those three variants.[144] While we're on *Too Loud a Solitude*, I should add that the first version was written in a kind of Apollinairesque verse, perhaps because I couldn't be bothered fussing about with punctuation, but maybe because when I saw the whole story, it was purely and simply in lyrical terms... But when I read the whole text for the first time, I found I had written it in Prague Czech, not slang, but vernacular. And then it suddenly dawned that my motif of the ordinary man, educated against his will, lacked irony, and that Prague irony would swim to the surface and would hit harder through the medium of standard Czech, through meticulously precise discourse. And so, quivering with excitement, I retuned and wrote the whole book again in the style I'd settled on. Whether in the heat of the moment or from innate indifference, I either shifted the text slightly away from the original or made some minor change, since I knew I couldn't spoilt it in any major way because it was a text I was afraid of, and when I'm afraid of a text, then at the very least it's a good one. And only after I re-read the whole version in 'proper' Czech did I see that it had gained not half an extra dimension, but a whole new dimension, so that only now was it an affecting story, since the intelligence in it could strike harder than a mere tale told in a tavern. So both *I served the King of England* and *Too Loud a Solitude* were written *alla prima*, like when a stopping train slowly passes from daylight

---

[144] The various versions of *Příliš hlučná samota* appeared in typescript (*samizdat*) editions in 1977 and 1978, and were first drawn together, also in a typescript edition (of 20 copies only), in 1986.

into a very long tunnel, or a deep dark night. Both are texts that I'm afraid to read; I'm even afraid to look at a single page. For one thing, I'm already somewhere else now, and my past texts – it's not that I loathe them, more than that, they're indifferent to me; it's not that I don't like talking about them, but I dislike answering admiring questions. They make me squirm and I even get embarrassed. A writer, and I suppose I am one, should treat his texts mercilessly – after all, the motifs that lie ahead are stronger than those I've left behind; a writer should have the courage to go on to where he is going to be afraid again, where no one expects him to be, where the present is non-existent, the past ominous and the future so very, oh, so very familiar, as my beloved György Lukács taught me...

Too Loud a Solitude *also reminds the reader that modern human communication is in a period of inflation. It forces man to return to Nature, which he has abandoned and restructured in a way that isn't even human. Mr Hrabal, what do you do when you see tears or when you find yourself on the brink of tears because of a breakdown in communication?*

I ascertain the cause of the tears and I weep with those who weep. I laugh with the crazy and with those who laugh, but when I see someone crying, I immediately have that same induced sensation or experience. I probably know what has happened to the person who is crying, so I try to fathom it, but I feel like crying as well, and when I find that there really is a reason for the tears, I start snuffling and – well – I get the tears too. You know, even good music, for example, Mahler's symphonies or Schubert, can bring tears to your eyes, but you have to listen to it alone or with someone you love a great deal. Music, what we call profound and fateful music – you know Chaikovsky's *Symphonie pathétique*, or Mahler's *Tragic Symphony* – they can make you feel just like a cow whose calf is being taken away from her. You feel like crying, and you can almost burst into tears at the cruelty of the human lot, but at the same time it lets you find something new in that cruelty. Mahler himself would invariably say that the hero of his first symphony, and his second, finds that satisfaction in death; only in death does he become victorious. There probably is no other way. This is what was felt by this typical Middle-European born in Kalište near Jihlava, who brought to a peak those tendencies that proceed from Schubert and Liszt and Wagner.

Do you cry often? When did you last cry?

Very often. Very often. Deep emotion from whatever source mists my eyes, because they are full of tears. Tears of joy arising from the great good fortune that I have been a witness to something or read something. Literature also brings about a light misting of my eyes. When you've grasped a particular essence, a truth, and you are travelling down the road that is being narrated – and it doesn't matter if it's by word or music – it usually ends, or culminates, more or less tragically. Mahler calls it *Auferstehung im Tode*, resurrection in death. In the *Eroica* the sense of the heroic brings you to ecstasy, leading you into an inchoate vale of tears, but they aren't ordinary tears – they're tears of the kind of joy you get from love or having being deeply touched. Most lovers also shed tears at their good fortune or at the peak of their happiness; tears are simply the response to supreme relations. Tears are in a way a typical element of Slav-ness. The old Russians always enjoyed a good weep, they would even have mild forms of choleric passion, rising to fits of tears. Most of Dostoyevsky or Chekhov's heroes melt into tears. They weep for joy, they weep from discovery, no matter whether it is death or love that they have discovered. It all goes together, love and death and futility and happiness and unhappiness – it all lies together in such a way that the transition, the rhythm, evokes one and the same response. It isn't the mystery of tears, no mystery. We have no reason for concealing our tears. When I weep, I weep. Like Hidegkuti when one of his pirouettes didn't work out.

The ancient Greeks did not cry very much.

They didn't have any reason to, because in their case everything came from without, and that means it happened by fate. They were more likely to be amazed at the mechanism into which they were dragged, and the moment they recognised that this was their fate, something that had come from without, that the gods had so decreed, they began to be dead before they'd actually died. So that's quite another matter. My impression is that they don't weep until there is a change of the transcendental firmament, when the subject is responsible for his own destiny and for the fate of others. So it isn't divine ordinance, but simply the fate which man himself has chosen. With that invariably comes a measure of the pathological and I think Goethe and Schiller both wrote about that. Or take

Orestes – and the early Lukács wrote about this – old Orestes is crazed by his own inflamed ideas. And that is where we find the start of modern drama, which culminates in Ibsen. In Ibsen people don't cry so much. But let's leave Ibsen – I was talking about the mystery of tears that we find among the Russians, the Slavs, and I too am a Slav. You'll find the mystery of tears in, say, Esenin. Esenin is that handsome chap who knows how to cry, who knows the mystery of tears, who wept his way from drunkenness and poetry to double suicide. So there you have him, one of my *poètes maudits*. My own fate is apparently different, but whenever I run up against a story I sense that the mystery of tears is a specifically Slav matter. The Poles like a good cry, with good reason mind you, but at the same time they are a proud people. You see, what's interesting about the Poles is that even if they suffer a defeat, they remain victors, because they bring down the curse of God – and that's why they're believers – on the victor, the one who caused their defeat. In other words, God is to exact revenge from him for all the wars and battles they've lost. That's why Chopin is so beautiful. Beautiful, no, that's a bad label, it's a vale of tears. Chopin... When it starts, I'm on the brink of tears, and the mazurkas – they're something to make you dance as Neruda danced with that beautiful girl who had to pop back home because her mother had died.[145]

---

[145] The reference here is to 'U tří lilií' (The Three Lilies, 1876), one of Jan Neruda's *Tales from the Little Quarter*, in which the narrator dances with a beautiful girl at the Three Lilies tavern. She is fetched by another girl, comes back after quarter of an hour and explains her absence with the simple sentence: 'My mother's just died.'

You have said that one and the same moment can be marked by radiant light and tragedy.

Those tears, that emotion, the emotionality that's like a drunkard's – well, if there is any value in man's having some nobility, then it's here: in the fact that one is capable of being touched to tears in Nature, in an erotic relationship, even in the recognition that Fate has given you the thumbs down. And yet you know you are not crying for yourself. You even cry at the joy of having been honoured, of having discovered that there are higher goals, forces that may lead you to disaster, or to its opposite. To some form of victory which you consider – or at least I consider – a defeat.

So you reckon tears are a specifically Slav thing.

How can I put it? What's typical is in literature, where heroes have no qualms about crying. Dostoyevsky himself weeps like that. After all, he was a man who burst into tears so very often; and when he laughed they would tell him to cry instead. His way of laughing was like that of someone released from prison – people's hair would just stand on end. He better suited the role with wrinkles, with those tears ever in his eyes as if touched with emotion. And women cry too. With them it isn't a pejorative manifestation. It's a sign of a disturbed system; their first reaction is tears. But not the tears I've been talking about. If someone dies and we cry, that's a natural reaction. By tears I mean the tears that sit lightly on the borderline between ethics and æsthetics. The tears I mean are more *he*-tears, they're the male principle and male tears. I mean the tears of Heraclitus, the weeping of a philosopher. The ancient Scythians welcomed a birth with weeping and death with jubilation. Great folk!

Because Heraclitus also maintains that 'it is sensible to recognise that everything is the same' I would like to ask you about the counterpoint to crying, laughter. Is laughter really the same thing as tears?

Maybe, or almost, because ever since childhood I've enjoyed laughing, since I know how to cry as well. But once you're sitting in the cauldron of eternity all you can do is laugh. I might be feeling glum, down in the mouth, feeling sorry for myself, wallowing in self-pity, and suddenly it's all over – like when my mother stroked the gloom away from my brow – and I begin to smile. And it's all nothing! It really is just nothing, all those little aches and pains, those spooky fears in case you've said or done something that wasn't quite right in a situation in which there is not just you, that is, me, but others as well, that is, people. Then it comes as a miracle: that you can see the sky and promenade beneath it, striding along beneath that great upturned vessel with the sweet sensation that at that moment I am safe from all harm. And if it's nothing to do with me, I am saved, even at the cost of being run over by a tram. It's a glorious feeling, being filled with a smile, that blissful smile that you see on the faces of all Buddhist priests as they gaze on the smiling statue of the Buddha, who, as he contemplates his navel, turns right back to the first man, to the womb of the first mother who had no navel. So I enjoy laughing and smiling – I only have to see Lupino Lane and Ben Turpin and Harold Lloyd, and all those other kings of the slapstick classics, but most of all I still like the shorts they used to put on between the Gaumont newsreel and the main film. What you get there is laughter concentrated in a small space, something like the magic of footballers on an area the size of a postage stamp – like what Hidegkuti and Puskás[146] were so good at, like the performances of circus artistes, like anything that is played out in a compact time and space. Full-length films by the kings of comedy knock me out; I always enjoyed laughing until I writhed, until I had to take care not to die of laughing. And the same goes for crying. And since everything has its counterpoint, laughter is also more *he*-laughter, it's also a male principle. Yet, you know, those slapstick shorts sometimes give me more; they have the knack of perpetually returning, like favourite tunes, like the memory of a beloved face. Like Hidegkuti remembering those pirouettes of his...

The way you love all your beloved faces, the way you treat all your victories as defeats, you sometimes give me the impression of playing the posturer.

I ought to be a posturer, I ought to be a ladies' man, but I look life in the face just as I look at a beautiful woman – I only look at her once she's passed me by. Anything that comes towards me so disconcerts

---

[146] Ferenc Puskás (see Note 136) is, in Britain, probably the best-remembered member of the Hungarian national football team and known variously as 'little brother', 'the galloping major' and 'golden head'. His club appearances were for Kispest and Honvéd at home in Hungary, then for Real Madrid, hence perhaps Hrabal's affectionate references to that team elsewhere (see Note 85). He is the world's number two top scorer of all time and is described as the first bona-fide football superstar.

me, so overawes me, so bruises me with its beauty that I'm incapable of looking it in the eye. Anything coming towards me is stronger than me; I always need to recover, to come round from a light faint; and not just because of people. Take the moon, when it pops up over a new meadow it so disconcerts me that I'm incapable of looking at it; I have to look first to the left, then to the right and then, agitated beyond bounds, I look it in the eye only to drop my eyelids after a mere second, like if a beautiful woman has glanced at me and I just know that if she addressed me I'd start talking utter rubbish. It takes an age for me to settle down after my speech has been derailed. I'm just as likely to start flirting with the wind as it turns the silvery leaves, I'm just as covered in confusion by the sight of a beautiful pheasant, or a hind who gets politely to her feet if I surprise her as she lies there in my garden. My first inclination is to shoot away from the source of my emotion, run off and carry away with me the impression that ejaculates over me with love at first sight. It's the same when I spot a beautiful red-capped mushroom lurking beneath some birches, I immediately look elsewhere, I'm all a-quiver, so exciting is that first glimpse, so precious, much the same as an undulating field of wheat, or like spring cabbage, swathed in quicksilver, like stalks of fox-grass... I expect it's because at that first, love-born sight I am penetrated by the essence of what I am seeing. For a brief instant, for a second, I become, I break into what I have just seen. I ought to be a posturer, a ladies' man, yet I am just a meek lover, daunted by the beauty that comes towards me in whatsoever guise. Which is why I relish everything only when it's too late, when the quivering images have settled down. In exactly the same frightened way I look at myself in the mirror; it grows old with me and I cannot find in it a single trace of anything that might justify me in saying, of myself, that after all perhaps I should be, for myself, just a little bit of a posturer and swaggerer. *Docta ignorantia*...

I am forced by the things you have been speaking of to ask whether you believe that human cognition has any bounds or not.

No, it hasn't. And if it has, then it's in silence; you don't even know about it, and that's a mercy. It's a kind of leap, the sort of thing Lukács talks about. Mysticism. The mystic simply knows and doesn't need to find reasons. According to Lukács, the mystic ends with fusion, and the hero with a downfall. But neither is far from the other, since the lives of both have become fulfilled. Of course, those are the poles of human existence, as Lukács, my teacher, would have it. In return, I ought to live in such a way as to identify with him, since several times I've been in situations where... As a train-dispatcher I could have been shot just like my hero. In other words, there's the question of whether the gun was pointing at me, as in *Closely Observed Trains*. I've been in that situation, so I know what it is to be seconds away from death. But I also know that other feeling, the sense of fusion with nature, or with a beloved, but above all with nature. At moments like that I merge with it totally. As a sensation, it is unutterably delicious and brings tears to the eyes. But when I might have been shot and was a hero, I was struck calm with terror. Terror-stricken, oh so terror-stricken that I was as calm as that train-dispatcher who could have been shot by the SS-man on that closely watched train. And I was saved by Chance, which is the miraculous by another name...

But we were talking about whether or not there are frontiers to human knowledge.

There are those two frontiers: the world of the hero and that of the mystic.

So perfect knowledge of the world can only come to one who will have known mercy?

But it's not something you can report on. And if anyone does, then it's just froth, gibberish, or a single sentence, like Zen. Confused rambling, from the rational man's point of view. In other words a text of the kind saints, or the blessed, produce. It begins with Tertullian: *Credo quia absurdum est* – I believe because it is absurd,[147] so it's a contradiction in terms, and a contradiction *per se*, you could say. There's more of the same scattered about. Take Socrates: I know that I know nothing. It might be meant ironically, but for me as a man of the twentieth century it's spot on. Or in the sixth century A.D. my teacher, old Lao Tzu, says in one chapter of the *Tao-te Qing* 'to know how not to know is the supreme attainment', doesn't he? And, leafing on through the memory, we find Nicolaus Cusanus,[148] a

[147] Originally: 'Certum est quia impossibile est.' (*De Carne Christi*, 5). Even more frequently misquoted as 'Credo quia impossibile'.

[148] Nicolaus Cusanus, real name Nicolas Krebs (1401–64), early-Renaissance German theologist, philosopher and natural scientist. Basing his thought on Neo-Platonist and Christian ideas he arrived at a pantheistic natural philosophy of the universe as an infinitely developed divinity which has become

bishop and most enlightened man, and his supreme utterance: *Docta ignorantia* – learned ignorance, which is really the run-up to Kant's common denominator. What Kant first proved with his philosophy of *ohne Subjekt kein Objekt* – that objects simply do not exist; the *Ding an sich selbst* is beyond cognition, everything existing only in the subject where it is mirrored. We have to tag everything we think exists with the categories of space and time, or maybe other categories instead, in other words a subject. The question of cognition is a kind of leap – like Kierkegaard – which is a way, if you like, to understanding how to break into things, a way of leaping into the *Ding an sich selbst*. There are paths of mercy in all religions which have grasped this, and the rest is just rational, simply 100 + 1; you can go on and on for as long as you like, and reason goes round and round in circles. You happen upon a railway station, you have the capacity to buy a ticket, you can sort out all sorts of things, you yourself can handle that tape-recorder – it's a rational activity. Reason ensures we can work this here gadget we're talking into; but it isn't that male thing, what you're asking about people have been seeking for over twenty thousand years. The oldest records we have exist because men have wanted to know things. They use religious forms, sometimes rational forms, but they never get beyond the threshold. The only ones who can make the leap inside are those who are, as Christ put it, blessed for being poor in spirit, blessed lunatics. The blessed – to pick up on Dostoyevsky, who identifies with Christ – are those

infinitely encoiled in the individual. Man's microcosm is thus subordinate to the divine macrocosm, though man, through cognition, rises above it.

ordinary peasants, the people Dostoyevsky identifies with, and in his works you'll always find the true humble man, but never the intellectual from the landed gentry. And wherever an intellectual of the landed gentry *is* a protagonist, he inevitably meets a tragic end. He may even try to take his own life, like Stavrogin for example. As you read Stavrogin, as you read *The Demons*, you wish you were Stavrogin; the times he overstepped the mark! You'd like to be a Raskolnikov, or an Ivan Karamazov, and sometimes you are. We think we can apprehend everything through reason, after all, even human society and the State – we've even thought we could get the better of that too by reason, and reason... reason... reason... No. Everything is subject to rhythm. And we get back to the question we started with. Cognition. And it's an extremely delicate question, a male question. So, to the best of my knowledge, I've only had one chance to be like a hero, but I wasn't, though I do know what it's like because I've stared death in the face. The second phase, that mystical fusion, that's come to me on several occasions. And if I were to analyse it – do a critique of practical reason – it isn't that I would *know* it; the only thing I do know is that ever since childhood I've been bewitched by moonlit nights, moon-spangled nights, you know, the stars, the moon, and me outside in the brewery orchard, in a state of such complete fusion that I ceased to be. And little Immanuel Kant himself writes: Sometimes as I walk through an August night and am bewitched by the glitter of the stars... It's of an almost Romantic order, *Ich begreife das Unbegreifliche*, I apprehend the ineffable, and that's the starry night above me and the moral law within me. As I've already said, I'm a pupil and weanling of François Rabelais – of course, he couldn't have quoted Kant, but *Gargantua and Pantagruel* contains the totality of ancient wisdom, melted down into several hundred, or maybe several thousand of those after that colon where he appeals to the Greek and Roman philosophers, and even some of the orientals. I reckon the best bit of *Gargantua and Pantagruel* is where the court poets are comparing a certain Persian king to God and he replies: 'My lasanophoros denies it, the chamberpot under my bed denies it.' Understand? It's those little things that have nothing to do with mystical ecstasy. Since I know that Kant also walked through the night and merged into it, my own modest fusion as a child and as a boy, and sometimes even now, always takes on a kind of solidity; after all, I know that a head other than mine is also capable of thinking like this, having been smitten in the same way. And we are smitten; note that, I forgot to say it: it isn't speculation, but being smitten. So I would say that those ciphers that are signs of a higher reality, ciphers that tend towards the logos – God and Good and Evil – everything that tends at the very least towards the transcendental or the metaphysical, is just following some path of mercy. And mercy is actually also the courage to take that leap in order to get there. It seems to come from without. Like you're addressed by it. I would maintain that ciphers – and the mystery of ciphers according to Jaspers is also in this – that ciphers speak to you, not you to them; you are addressed and therein is the mercy, that you are addressed. *Fruitio dei...*

In my view, mercy comes to him who learns what beauty is, as defined by Simone Weil, the French philosopher: Beauty is a maze. If a man has the strength, he can reach the middle of the maze. There a god is waiting for him, he devours him, and then regurgitates him. At that point he leaves the maze, takes up a position near the entrance and amiably invites all passers-by to enter.

That's how Kafka's *Trial* ends as well. Josef K., come to me!

Speaking of Kafka and inclination: you have a law degree.

It's taken me a lot of time and effort to forget all that.

I know. So you've got a forgotten law degree. What's your view of the contrast between law – legal right – and inclination?

Law has been used to modify everything that was once inclination. Inclination is your self's inner right to do this or that even at the cost of becoming a wreck. Possibly even the wrecking of one's own self. It's inclination, it's longing, love, when poets are addressed from above showing that their heaven is appeased; and if they aren't, they founder. But even in that downfall, when they experience that he, that essence, which addressed them and caused them to founder exists, their heaven is appeased even in that fall. Prometheus's liver...[149]

---

[149] As a punishment, Zeus chained Prometheus – man's benefactor who taught him the use of fire and other useful arts previously reserved to the gods – to a rock on Mt Caucasus. During the day, an eagle consumed his liver, which was restored each succeeding night, the subject of Aeschylus's play, *Prometheus Chained*. Prometheus was thus exposed to perpetual torture. However, Hercules killed the eagle and, with Zeus's consent, saved the sufferer who thus gained immortal fame.

So in the words 'law', 'right' you sense aggression, or power-seeking?

That's another matter. We'd have to move on to the political sphere. Plato, perhaps one of the most glorious philosophers, a disciple of Socrates, treated law as higher than longing since at one moment he arrived at the proposition that poets – and Picasso also quotes this – should be driven out of the Republic by law-abiding citizens because they are detrimental to it. And Picasso adds: 'And quite right too. Which is why I praise the laws of the Academy, so that I can transgress them. And head off somewhere else.' In other words if you ignore the particular forms of social behaviour which the law lays down for you, you can become a Prometheus who steals fire... I have always tried to steal the fire, to breach injunctions and to create myself and my work, and my heaven has always been appeased. So there always has to be a certain set of laws, there have to be regulations, so that a man of courage can try to infringe them. Ovid too, unless I'm mistaken, sought after the forbidden. Although Prometheus knows he'll be punished, that the eagle will come and peck out his liver, he stole the fire from the gods, and that was the limit. He went against commands and prohibitions, he infringed taboos and, at some cost to himself, moved things forward. And that's the opposition between conservatism and innovation in the modern sense – seeking something new; and you know, it's even in the quite mundane facts of everyday life. So we might be said to be surrounded by those ordinary folk who often aspire to the forbidden and willingly transgress. I know, we all have it in us, that rebellion against convention, in both our erotic and our civic lives. Then of course there are those paramount individuals, like John Huss[150] – in the sphere of morality and religion, hence in a particular sphere of politics – who simply paid the price, just like Giordano Bruno.[151] Even the sublime Charles Baudelaire spent a year in gaol, accused of subverting public morality with his *Fleurs du Mal*. We know what befell Rembrandt when he exhibited his *Night Watch*;[152] we know what happened to the Impressionists when they held their first exhibition,[153] or how the Fauvistes fared at the Armory Show in the United States in 1913.[154] When European art arrived there, people went berserk; that was when America first realised that they're more than just cowboys and those brave guys played by Gary Cooper. At any time, anything new, anything that's too new, first causes a scandal and confusion, but eventually even it becomes

[150] Jan Hus (?1371–1415), the most important of the medieval Bohemian religious reformers, burned at the stake as a heretic in Constance; his life and works have considerable resonance among the Czechs to this day.

[151] Giordano Bruno (1548–1600), the great Italian (Dominican) thinker in whom Renaissance philosophy reached its peak. For his pantheistic views and his criticism of the contemporary Church he was persecuted, sent before the Inquisition and finally burned to death in Rome. A forerunner of such later philosophers as Spinoza, Leibniz and Herder.

[152] The more familiar name of Rembrandt's *Sortie of the Shooting Company of Captain Frans Banning Cocq* (1642).

[153] The exhibition was held in 1874 and was not a success; the Impressionists experienced much opposition.

[154] The Armory Show took place in New York at the armoury of the 69th regiment. It was arranged by The Eight group of independent artists, who were seeking freedom from the constraints of the National Academy and supported progressive trends in art. The show was the first major exposure of the American art world to Fauvism, Cubism and other Paris-based movements and had a major impact on American art and art criticism.

conventional, and so, for example, in the name of Impression people also condemned Expressionism. Yet there is no way of willing yourself to be progressive and modern, no. It has to be in your personality to provoke, and yet be innocent. I believe that's the way it has always been in thought and art.

Let's stay with law: what do you, as an ex-lawyer who has forgotten about the law, think of this: it seems to me that there is too much of a contrast in Machiavelli, who wrote not only poems and plays but also political works, and even formulated an idea which still seems to apply and to retain its attraction today: The centralised state is fine for winning power, but for the retention of power you need a republic.

The strong individual who knows he has plenty of support in a given society and is seeking to change something can select any means to achive his end. Machiavelli has attestations of this in *Il Principe*. I believe he had a precursor, a contemporary of Dante called Marsilius of Padua.[155] Sometime in 1325 he wrote *Defensor Pacis*, where he also codified the right to rebel against both the Pope and the Emperor. And ultimately it was he, this Marsilius of Padua, who laid the foundations for revolution and the overthrow of feudal dualism by the bourgeoisie. The last chapter's where you'll find the right to rebel; in other words, Marsilius provided a fully-fledged philosophical foundation for the new, bourgeois society, for the towns – Florence, against the feudal lords and above all against

[155] Marsilius of Padua (c.1280–1342) argued that the Church should be regulated by the secular authorities and not meddle in government. His *Defensor Pacis* actually appeared in 1324.

the dualism of Emperor and Pope, because the towns had become a new political reality. The new society got its ethical foundations from Marsilius of Padua, and what Machiavelli did in *Il Principe* was to elaborate on it. I can't say, but if Machiavelli had lived in Bohemia and had been able to trace the development of the reign of the Přemyslide dynasty, who won power by the mass murder of the Slavník family – we recently marked its thousandth anniversary[156] – well these Přemyslides could have provided ample material for *Il Principe*, because they did the same thing. For them, murder, or gouging out a brother's eye, that was no problem. The Slavník's were a milder lot, which is why they were caught napping. The Přemyslides always had plenty of brutality and mettle, but Charles IV outdid even the Přemyslides in cruelty; his cruelty knew no bounds. *Der letzter Universalist auf dem Thron...* as Hegel accurately described our beloved Father of the Nation...[157]

[156] The Slavníks held most of Bohemia east of the Vltava. They got into conflict with the Přemyslide prince Boleslav II, whose men then captured their main seat at Libice nad Cidlinou in 995 and slaughtered every Slavník they found there.

[157] 'Father of the Nation', the popular nickname of Charles IV (1316–78), hints at the pious respect in which he is widely held by the Czechs (he is the Charles of Charles Square, Charles Bridge and Charles University in Prague). The 'ruthless' aspect of his rule plays little part within the national mythopoeia that shapes the king-emperor's surviving image. Without it, however, he could barely have achieved all that he did in consolidating the dominant position of Bohemia in medieval Europe, by edict, negotiation and a string of diplomatic marriages. The nickname was first applied by Vojtěch Raňkův z Ježova (d. 1388) in his funeral oration.

And what if a cruel individual changes the law?

That's the very thing with *Il Principe*! That's perhaps how it is. But when Baudelaire wanted to change forms, he probably proceeded just as brutally against the verse of the classics, just as mercilessly, as Machiavelli's Prince; those same Medicis really were brutal beyond measure. My feeling is that a poet must be just as brutal if he wants to move things forward; not when he feels like it, but when the time is ripe.

The brutality of lyrical verse and the brutality of politics – I wouldn't place them on the same plane.

No, not the same. But there are similarities, at least for me. Even the statesman sometimes works with people, groups of people, mercilessly and brutally, just as the poet with his subject matter and his heroes. At the start of this conversation we said: Where there is a father, there is a pyramid, and at the top of the pyramid is *Il Principe*, who asserts his will so totally that if anyone gets in his way he will remove them. Freud wrote the same thing in *The Future of an Illusion*. I believe the idea was taken further forward in the United States by Herbert Marcuse. I was sitting with him once at a Hegel symposium in Albach and we were chatting about this. When will wars cease? When we are all sons. As soon as a father appears, there you'll have *Il Principe*. It forms the very basis of Marcuse's philosophy, which is why he so inspired left-wing, Marxist-leaning young people in the 1960s. Over a beer I asked him – since it was a Hegel conference – whether, if Hegel were alive, he might not view sport as one of those categories in which the absolute spirit is manifest. As in religion, philosophy and art. But sport appeared in a way unknown to Hegel. And sport is on the way to replacing religion. In his days, sport did not fire the masses. For me, top-flight football matches are like the Mass! And Marcuse laughed, then said: 'Ja, mein lieber Herr.' Yes. And he was even surprised he hadn't hit on the problem himself, that it was a fabulous question, the way I had formulated it over a pint. Beer again. It wasn't far from Innsbruck, at Albach, he was running the conference. I'd been invited along as well, to listen in and listen up, and I had been directing my attention to consuming enormous quantities of Innsbruck beer, and we used to drink *Obstler* with it. As he passed he sat down with us. And I could tell he had no problem downing six Innsbruck lagers. To say nothing of my seeing in him a resemblance to Goethe, a hugely handsome man, with a robust, athletic physique, and that Goethe nose. Romain Rolland called Goethe a melancholy bull. He knew how to handle women, you know. Like Hidegkuti... And women would even write him thank-you letters...

How many people have you known who were – how should I put it? – above and beyond you?

I've known several such people, and I'm duly grateful. Having arrived in Prague I came to know Egon Bondy, a poet, but as a philosopher he calls himself Zbyněk Fišer; he knows Sanskrit, he knows what Zen Buddhism is; as a young man, and for his own purposes, he was the first to translate Christian Morgenstern.[158] Then Vladimír Boudník[159] turned up, and

Jiří Kolář[160] and Jiří Weil.[161] So I have met the kind of people who knew how to pass on everything to me, even things from the past, so educated were they. For example Kolář read Shakespeare every year. I've never heard anything more beautiful about Shakespeare than from Jiří. Because there's a direct line from Shakespeare to Joyce. Then from Joyce to Eliot. Eliot, that *Wasteland*, owns much to an inner kinship with Joyce's *Ulysses*. And when I was young, there was this apparently unknown painter, Antonín Frýdl.[162] That man, who lived in utter penury, introduced me to Kant. It was thanks to him that I began, at the age of twenty-one, to study metaphysics.

Those friends of yours would go that little street in Libeň, Na hrázi. Did you learn a lot from them?

When I moved there, I was young, and one of them, Vladimír Boudník, already lived there, and Mr Marysko,[163] and later, with the passage of time, Ivo Tretera[164]

[158] Christian Morgenstern (1871–1914), German experimental (nonsense) poet.

[159] See Note 86.

[160] See Note 53.

[161] Jiří Weil (1900–1959), Czech journalist, novelist and translator from Russian. Better remembered for his novels on the fate of the Jews than as author of the first Czech novels about Stalinism.

[162] Antonín Frýdl (1896–1975), figurative and landscape artist, who spent many years in Nymburk. He shared all Hrabal's loves of football, beer and movements in twentieth-century art (Surrealism, Dadaism, Poetism).

[163] See Note 134.

[164] Ivo Tretera (b. 1933), a long-term friend of Hrabal's, interested in the theory of cognition and the philosophy of education. He shared Hrabal's interest in Surrealism and abstract art. Like many others in this mould he was removed from his university post during the 'Normalisation' of the 1970s, but was reinstated in 1989 (Professor of the History of Philosophy since 1995; see htttp://www.phil.muni.cz/fil/scf/komplet/tretera.titul).

would visit No.24, and Dr Zumr,[165] and we didn't just do weddings, huge wedding breakfasts, but we also discussed philosophy and man's last extremity, with much laughter. It was there that I wrote my first books, I married and lived there with my wife Pipsi. The stage-hands from the nearby Stanislav Kostka Neumann Theatre would come and visit, also the Vávra brothers[166] and Mr Buřil,[167] Surrealist workmen, and the unforgettable Jiří Šmoranc,[168] a varnisher who liked nothing more than to talk about André Breton and Jacques Vaché,[169] into whom he projected himself. They all wrote; we used to go to read notices of forthcoming marriages and if we liked a bride's name, we would hold a wedding at the house in her honour. We'd have roast pork and drink lashings of beer from Vaništa's pub, and once we got into the mood we would read out our texts; Dr Zumr would talk about Heidegger or Jaspers, and our favourite reading matter was Lao Tzu – just one sentence, a different one

[165] See Note 52. Several of Zumr's photographs appear in Josef Tomeš's *Libeňskou minulostí* (Prague-Libeň, 2001), helping to conserve an image of this place that meant so much to Hrabal. Zumr's house, like Hrabal's, was a regular meeting place for the people mentioned in this part of the conversation.

[166] Stanislav (b. 1933) and Vladimír Vávra (??); the former, a printer and lover of French modern poetry, was himself a poet and dramatist of the 'Libeň group' and a friend of Vladimír Boudník, in whose street-art performances he regularly played a part. Vladimír Vávra is a radio mechanic and novelist.

[167] Zdeněk Buřil (??), an admirer of André Breton and the Surrealists generally; himself a poet in the Surrealist mode.

[168] Jiří Šmoranc, a painter and decorator and poet. Along with several of the others mentioned on this page, Hrabal habitually mentions him in the list of visitors to his Libeň house, but information on many of them is hard to come by. Even Josef Tomeš in *Libeňskou minulostí* (note 165), while listing a dozen familiar names (p.87), offers no guide to these lesser known figures.

[169] Jacques Vaché (1895–1919, suicide), a writer who is associated with the French Dadaists and influenced Breton in particular.

every time, and that kept us going all evening. Because the sun could never shine into the flat, I would haul a chair and a little table all round the yard, and I would even seek the sun on the shed roof, which caught its warmth at setting. There I had a divan and a chair with the legs cut down to compensate for the slope of the roof; I even had two chairs because I used one to write on; I wrote on a *Perkeo* typewriter, a superb machine, a German portable dating back to the *Sezession*, which had no Czech accents. Because one time my brother left his St Bernard with me, I had the yard full of local boys, and the St Bernard loved kids and they loved him. It was summertime and we would dress him in swimming trunks and the boys would take him across the main road, across the bridge, down to the river, where we went swimming. I even wrote about it, that the street was really on the dyke of eternity,[170] also for the reason that whoever lived in that little house with a yard, in the front part, which had an upper storey, everyone was called Mr Fiala. Because the house had belonged to a Mr Fiala – paints and dyes – so everyone was called Mr Fiala; I too was Mr Fiala, Vladimír Boudník was Mr Fiala, everyone...

This means that in the 1950s that house was quite notorious – 24 Na hrázi.[171]

Let me tell you a story: in that house we never locked up at night and so on several occasions a drunk

---

[170] The street's real name, *Na hrázi*, means 'on the dam' or 'dyke'; 'on the dyke [or 'brink'] of eternity' is a pun on *hráz* that does not have quite the same ring in English.

[171] Szigeti is right, and it remained notorious for as long as it was associated with Hrabal and his circle of friends. It disappeared in 1988 as part of a slum-

came in, lay down and fell asleep. Only in the morning did we discover that we didn't even know the man. The house was probably also notorious for being permanently open, just like the people who lived there. On one famous occasion, when my brother and sister-in-law and my wife and I were asleep, someone came in in the small hours, it was still dark, and started feeling our faces and my wife was scared witless. I put the light on and there was this middle-aged drunken woman standing there, and she gave me three hundred crowns and asked for my signature; the money was for the baby, from the trade union, and she had been scouring the pubs for me all night. Another time a drunk came in after midnight and asked us to pour him a drink because Horkýs' in the Jewish quarter[172] had closed and they'd told him that they'd stopped serving and the only place he could drink all night was at Fiala's. He was wheezing because he was holding a 'nightingale', you know, a kind of vent, in place at his throat with one finger. And so I would get up, open the door, and see people out, and go conscientiously to work and yet have time for nocturnal conversations and my friends. I would say that in those days I lived on the dyke of eternity, but nowadays all those things I lived through would be the death of me. I tire easily, I can't sit for more than two or three hours at one go, I'm simply exhausted sometimes. But as Novalis put it: we have our memories, that second now.

clearance programme. A photograph of the rear view, from the yard that meant so much to Hrabal, can be found in Tomeš's *Libeňskou minulostí*, p.86.
[172] In the nineteenth century Libeň had a small, compact Jewish quarter by the river; its presence survives in toponyms, one of which, *v Židech*, is what Hrabal uses here.

But Mr Hrabal, you keep flitting about, escaping, talking about something else. Do please tell me: do you love your nation?

Flitting about... but that's my style, you remember I wanted our dialogue to have a few sentences from Hašek's *Schweik* as an epigraph? – 'Have you been swimming in the Malše? – No, but there could be a good crop of plums this year...' As for loving my nation. I don't even know... perhaps through writing. I think I do like people since I've been giving myself out to them these fifty years, my door's ever open, for fifty years I've been giving myself out to them in pubs, I think I love my nation because I cut down the difference between ordinary mortals and intellectuals... because I don't differentiate between myself and other people. But as I've said, those were the good old days. Now, after fifty years of giving myself out, I'm tired, I'm pretty much down, but I don't complain because the great beauty of writing is that no one *has* to do it, but now I'm feeling a bit groggy, see... I've out-pirouetted myself on my postage stamp...

That doesn't surprise me in the slightest, Mr Hrabal... Okay, so you do like people, that much follows from your hominism. But how do you think one should love one's nation?

I can only speak for myself... My love for my nation comes out of my love for the environment in which I live with those others. It's in my devout relationship to language, to my native tongue, slangs and jargons, the *hantec*[173] of Brno, the city where I grew up... But my

---

[173] The unique urban dialect of Brno, of which its users are intensely proud. It is barely intelligible to the outsider and not all the locals have a full command of its lexical richness. Prague has nothing to compare with it.

love for my nation is also in my having worked hard for over a quarter of a century, in having accepted more responsibilities than asserted any rights... And it's in my having written, having dared to write things that are not spoken... This is why I love everything connected with my Czech mother tongue and its earthy language, everything that makes it what it is... I am loving this nation as I attempt to mould, in my own way, all that is anonymous, ridiculous or even tender in what I have seen and heard about me... I try patiently to convert that multidimensional reality into the one-dimensional lines on my typewriter, my typescript, by which I seek to celebrate the vernacular, because the speech of ordinary people is my language, too. Which is why there lives, in my linguistic hostelries, among my people, an anonymous Oscar..., why through its kind of brilliance my language gives me such flashes of magnificence, such delicate titbits. Have you ever noticed that jokes, anecdotes, have never been thought up by intellectuals? Sandburg once attempted to write a book of them, and foundered. Even Sandburg. It must be the anonymous masses, those anonymous people, who have a kind of spontaneous command of language as a higher-order signalling system that lacks rationality. For the poet, folk-song is the acme, it's beyond his reach. The folk anecdote is anonymous, beyond your reach. Certain rituals and customs, which can be quite brutal, such as Easter whippings,[174]

---

[174] This is a reference to the folk custom whereby Czech men beat the women with plaited willow switches on Easter Monday, to be rewarded with painted eggs. The word, *pomlázka*, refers not only to the custom itself, but also to the switch and the 'reward'.

birth, marriage, funerals, they all have a ritual quality to them which you can't invent, because they have been perpetuated by the passing centuries. Mark you though: Hegel has one wonderful sentence: 'Better is the man who expresses himself better...' And remarkably, we have here this nation which lives through its anonymous creations, its artefacts – say painted linenchests. Ultimately you can derive everything from the people. As for me, I can derive all my writing, my real, my best ideas from things I've heard, things I've had donated. I have been addressed – what we were saying earlier, that cipher, those transcendental locales, have to speak to you. Only then have you been smitten and honoured by the grace of being in a mystical state, that you are who you are, that you are an identity. But I'm not going to talk just about art; you have the same thing with human speech, the mother tongue. You know that full well yourself. Everything is within the folk I live among. I've never been like you, for example, whose very job it is to ask questions deliberately. I'm just one of them – they might be kind to me or not, I'm just there and I'm one of them, but when I get home, I get a sudden prickling in my head – I've heard something that I've never heard before. Or I've heard an anecdote that we don't know who thought up – no author to it. Fortunately, things were no different in Gothic art: the things that truly break your heart and mind in the Gothic are all anonymous... But today, anyone who daubs a picture, or writes a piffling poem, or makes a silly little statue – they all start getting big ideas...

So how does one love one's nation? Love one's language?

Love one's nation? In my own view, my nation has every conceivable vice, but it also has its virtues, and that's creativity, creative powers, thinking up anecdotes, inventing slangs, coming up with new syntaxes, breaking the rules of language, breaking conventions – it's all in those people. And so I am one of them, I'm just the usher into the common denominator, just a recorder, like Božena Němcová when she collected her fairy-tales; she so loved her nation.

Pilinszky[175] also said of the Gothic that we don't know who created it; no one signed his name, we just have their cathedrals and other works. So literature and the writer will also recede into anonymity, since…

So it should be, since what is important isn't *who* wrote something, but *what* he wrote! I'm not a writer, I'm a recorder. I've been saying that for ages. Down with the cult of personality…

Let's have another go at that great game of ours, to refresh ourselves. What comes to mind when I say the word – bliss?

Chest… You're rubbing my chest. I do it as well; when I'm feeling blissful I rub my chest like this. But that doesn't matter. We agreed – the first word that comes to mind. Chest!

Eyes.

Dots.

---

[175] János Pilinszky (1921–81), Hungarian poet of a meditative lyricism.

Trust.

Exhalation. Heaving a sigh. Two halves that have found each other.

Poet.

Tree, but a spreading tree. And eyes in the wrong place...

Pharisee.

Impostor. The sight of me in a mirror...

Impostor.

Away... Away from that. That's me...

Inclination.

Head to head. First love... Lovers...

Universe.

A hand gesture... Let there be light... Repent...

Bread.

Life... Man is what he eats... Schelling.

Border.

A line.

That's the same thing. OK, line.

The limit beyond which I can't go. Limit. Break-up and passing-by...

And emotion.

A sigh... An eye imprinted in a counter-eye, a hand in a hand...

Grace.

Bliss. Being drowned in feathers scattered from wings...

Table.

Flat space. White space...

Space?

You know, a surface. Lit from above, a table-cloth and clasped hands resting on it.

You strike me as an atheist, yet you're still looking for a god. What does this paradox mean?

Look here, my friend... For pagans ignorant of the faith, the truth...

Aren't I spot on?

Yes. Descartes spells out the reason for his thinking; and what does he say? I doubt, therefore I am. Only an atheist can arrive at what God is. Only negation can discover the positive. So you have to work your way towards it. By harbouring doubts about God you almost instate him; He's there, you are already recognising His existence... You have your doubts about Him, but there He is.

So by the very fact of doubting I'm finding the divine anchor?

Yes. It's always an excess of intellect, an excess of *cogito*. But the atheist at least recognises God, since he allows for his possible existence. When I see a beautiful table, I infer that someone made it.

Pilinszky has said that a writer must live in a friendly atmosphere. If he has no friends, no friendly atmosphere, he cannot create the truth, he cannot write...

That's right. He must have one friend. We must have at least one person to identify with, to lean on.

One person... Right now my impression is that you incline towards metaphysics, that...

I think that only music can capture everything. Music does have something metaphysical about it; music is capable of finding a way into extreme situations, into love, your mood, dying; music can even be used to express a world outlook, just as much as a book or painting. Today I know that any change of transcendental locales is the essence of change in music, that no work of music could ever be produced unless history and philosophy showed, on the clock of Time, a turning-point in social affairs.

Do you play any musical instrument?

I learned to play the piano and as a student I played trumpet in an orchestra, just an ordinary E-flat trumpet, but I also played the piano. More for my own pleasure though, or because that's what you did in those days. I played regularly at the *Pod mostem* pub; I had sheet music in Nymburk, so in those days I would always play Strauss waltzes and the hits of the day. I used to tinkle away, making plenty of mistakes, a bit like how I write today...

Was it your livelihood?

No, it was just evenings. For a bit of light relief. My big successes were playing the odd Chopin nocturne or Liszt's *Liebestraum*, but at the same time – as you've seen, it's been with me since childhood – I enjoyed growing vegetables.[176] We had a garden at the brewery and I was forever doing a spot of hoeing. My hands got cramped from the spade and shovel or those mattocks, sort of stiffish, so I wasn't quite as good on the piano as I had been, and actually gave it up later. But I was still fond of music. The school at Nymburk was unique in that one chemistry teacher insisted that seventh-grade pupils should be allowed to choose between descriptive chemistry or music. So obviously I chose music. I had two classes a week regularly that year, normal lessons they were, and the marks counted. The music teacher had gramophone records and she improved us by teaching us musical forms, so in the course of that year of musical education and guidance I fell in love with Beethoven, Wagner, Smetana. We even used to go to Prague to the opera, so my enjoyment of music survives to this day. That time you came to see me at Kersko, my daughter had brought me Mahler's Fifth from Germany; she'd phoned to ask what she could bring me and I'd asked her for that Mahler symphony. And so I shall continue to discover music I don't yet know or only have an inkling of. Just as I had wept over Schubert or Chaikovsky as a teenager, I also loved *L'après-midi d'un Faune*. Those days, in my twenties, I loved Debussy; it seemed to go with Nymburk – there were still those gigantic poplar trees that they'd

---

[176] This is probably another instance where a previous reference, this time to growing vegetables, has disappeared in the editing process.

planted along the river. I lived in an area that seemed absolutely cut out for the Impressionists. You had everything there. And music of course. But without Debussy I wouldn't have heard it.

Was there any one captivating musical experience in your youth?

But of course. Beethoven's Fifth. That symphony quite simply showed me what can be said with music, that even grand ideas can be said. Even Destiny itself, which comes from without, and you sort of become almost its plaything. Of course, not the kind of plaything that means you can't fight back and at least try to compete with fate – in the sense that you know what's happening to you and how you might get the better of it, even though it is getting the better of you. Because a man who knows that he is borne along by fate is, relatively speaking, no worse off than others, but at least he has the sense that there *are* forces that can be called fate. And then, in effect, they determine your future. Anyone who has recognised the power of fate is also giving it the nod, because you've recognised the frontiers, the limits of human possibilities and the point at which the realm of God, or higher forces, begins. And so music, Beethoven, all nine symphonies – we gradually went through them all at school, and I was profoundly affected; but as I listen to them now during the Prague Spring festival... Another thing: I like listening to Radio Vienna. And from eleven o'clock onwards, daily from eleven to twelve, Vienna broadcasts the best orchestras, the best conductors, the best soloists, and it lasts a whole hour.

So it's safe to say that you had a good musical education in your youth. And what's music like at Czech schools nowadays?

I can't say. I don't have any children to bring me reports on what goes on in school, but as far as I'm aware, the interest in music is far greater than it was in my day. Wherever you go today, everywhere... recorded music.

Even greater?

Even greater. These days, when tape-recordings of symphonies come out, or tapes of such as the Beatles or other famous artists, Count Basie,[177] the American jazz number one, or Mahler's symphonies, they sell out at the record shops and elsewhere in the blinking of an eye. Wherever you go, you're met by recorded music.

Do you like jazz?

Of course. Not that I'm what you might call a... For me jazz reaches its peak in Count Basie, with his chubby fingers and fantastic blues style. For me he's the tops. I know there is also Elvis Presley, but I like other sorts of best-sellers, black music...

Louis Armstrong.

Armstrong is another one that's everything to me. He makes mistakes singing, he makes mistakes on the trumpet, but those mistakes are hugely human. His voice is so ordinary, human, like when someone is singing in great sorrow, or again in great euphoria, and he

[177] Surprisingly, for a man of Hrabal's interests, *Basie* is consistently spelled with two *s*'s.

sort of sings just for himself. Whether in a bar, slightly drunk – or very, and his voice is the kind that invigorates, and sometimes it brings tears to my eyes. That gravelly voice – and then he picks up his trumpet, that trumpet of his and lets go, it's… I even saw him live, he came to Prague and I was dazzled by him for ever and ever. To me he's a true artist and absolutely identical to the Armstrong of those days when he played with King the king[178] in New Orleans… Like Hidegkuti and Ferenc Puskás.

Do you ever sing? I ask because I once asked my mother why she sang when she was on her own at home, and she replied: 'So as not to be alone.' Do you sing?

No. I sometimes whistle a bit, or when I do sing, I sing – if you like – kind of deliberately out of tune. These days I can't sing the way I used to when I was young, when I went with the lads down to the river, after dusk, in Nymburk, when we would sing with great feeling such songs as 'It was a beautiful night in May', 'Our oars are long, our boat is short', or vice versa: 'Our boat is long and the oars are short, come my beloved…'.[179] We just knew one another as people and so we – those ordinary lads and I – would always

---

[178] Doubtless a reference to Joe 'King' Oliver (1885–1938), who is described as 'acting as a father to Louis'.

[179] The first of these songs is *Byla noc krásná*, a conventional song of nostalgia for frustrated young love, ending with the enjoinder to the inconstant beloved to come and visit the singer in his dark grave, but not to weep too much. The original version of the second song is the second wording suggested here by Hrabal (long boat, short oars); it is a typical pre-war, quasi-'country' campfire evergreen of the kind sung by those given to such outdoor pursuits as canoeing, rafting, hiking or camping and is to be heard sung in the film version of Hrabal's *Postřižiny* (Cutting it Short).

spend an hour or two singing like that with such tremendous feeling whenever it was a nice evening. Of course I know it was a time when there was singing everywhere. As I returned to the brewery I would always hear our maltsters singing; their voices carried across the orchard all the way to the house. People used to sing as they worked. Or the coopers. But chiefly the maltsters. On my way to school from the brewery I had to cross a field, and at Zálabí, on the other side of the river, by the bridge, there was a joinery, and as I trotted by at quarter past seven in the morning, stepping on it to get to school by seven-thirty – the joiners would be singing.

But these days people don't sing.

People don't sing any more. Mind you, these days it looks as if people do hardly anything at all. I'm from a town where there used to be five theatres. Nymburk. Today there is only one, but thank God for it. But there were villages, tiny villages and small towns, with dramatics going on everywhere. Today there's none of that, and no singing. Why should people bother? If you put the radio on you've got those flashy types doing the singing for you, people like Karel Gott and Ivan Mládek[180] for a start, and you're pushed aside. Or theatre: you put the television on and the best of the best will play you some... Bratislava – you know the plays they always put on every Monday. Here in Prague we always looked forward to those Slo-

---

[180] Karel Gott (b. 1939), a perennial Czech crooner, whose popularity extends to Germany; Ivan Mládek (b. 1942) a writer and banjo-band leader and performer of satirical songs on every conceivable topic.

vak drama productions on Mondays, they were top-notch.[181] So why would you do a play when you can see the best theatre at home, from your own armchair – and have a smoke or a beer while you watch. It's obvious! Though there are some clever folk, people who've grown a bit bored with it, jaded enough to start rehearsing productions of their own. People are beginning to appreciate the mystery, the beauty of putting on their own play. They may not be so good as the professionals, that goes without saying, but they're doing their own drama thing. So it's slowly reviving, coming back. Or some people come together to form their own quartet. Or enjoy a game of football on a bit of spare ground. There's a revolution going on today.

Did you ever play chamber music at home?

No, we didn't do that. For one thing we weren't up to it, and for another, we had one of the first gramophones, and that introduced me to the voices of Enrico Caruso or Ema Destinn.[182] But at the same time – thanks to my father's own passion – I discovered humour on gramophone records, people like Vlasta Burian.[183] Or the comedy of Fanda Mrá-

---

[181] Hrabal is by no means alone in this response to Slovak television drama, which was perfectly accessible to the Czech viewer as well, given the closeness between the two languages. This is a perhaps peripheral and ephemeral contribution of the Slovaks to Czechoslovak culture, but one not to be overlooked. Any more than the contemporaneous contribution to translated literature; the Slovak publishing houses were often more agile in this respect than the Czech.
[182] Ema (Emmie) Destinn(ová) (1878–1930), the Czech operatic soprano who achieved considerable success in Berlin, at Covent Garden and the New York Metropolitan Opera.
[183] Vlasta Burian (1891–1962), actor and comedian in cabaret and the mainstream theatre and star of numerous Czech comic film classics.

zek[184] or Jára Kohout.[185] I got carried away with Fanda Mrázek, and I know some of his recordings almost by heart. They're in my head, where they became implanted and made me ecstatic. That record where he starts: 'I was stupid enough to be born in Žižkov.'[186] Told in that voice of his. It had me in stitches and the same fits of laughter as when I saw Charlie Chaplin.

You've mentioned Mahler, Chopin, Beethoven, Smetana...

Mr Szigeti, you're asking me questions as if I was some sort of expert... and I'm not. The questions you ask are making me tread on thin ice... I know we agreed that I would also answer questions about things I don't know much about, and what smatterings I know I'd let you have... but – let's be a bit tactful... a moment back I was talking about Vlasta Burian and Fanda Mrázek, and now you're going on about geniuses. All I can say is that for me Smetana means... *Má vlast*... then purely and simply *The Bartered Bride*... an opera that makes me afraid, an opera whose very melancholy makes me grip my heart and burst into tears... and I have to take care in case I nearly die. Whenever I listen to *The Bartered Bride* on the radio or TV in Kersko, it's more or less okay... because if I do start choking at the music and singing I can run out into

[184] Fanda (František) Mrázek (1903–70), comic actor in film and cabaret, associated with operetta and himself the author of three operettas.
[185] Jára Kohout (1904–94), Czech comic actor (theatre and film) and theatre proprietor and director. He spent the years of Communism in the USA, returning home in 1990. His film career stretched from *Venoušek a Stázička* (V and S, 1922) to a cameo appearance in *Ještě větší blbec, než jsme doufali* (A bigger fool than we hoped, 1994); he was most prolific in the 1930s.
[186] Žižkov was one of the large working-class districts on the fringe of central Prague.

the woods as far as the brook... and there I can let the tears flow without feeling embarrassed... with the *Bride* things have gone so far that I might almost run off in anticipation... that opera has something more to it, an entire extra dimension... something that only a Czech can understand, not with the intellect, but with some second sense. A Czech who is graced by still having what it takes, by being capable of so much emotion that he might almost wish to be caught out by its melancholy beauty so badly that he could die... And Dvořák? More of the same. His quartets... they're like ground glass, they're something else I can only listen to in Kersko so I can escape in time to the brook and have a good cry in the darkness... his other music, ground glass again, and those few melancholy *Slavonic Dances*... again I rise to my feet, wring my hands and run out and wail out loud... I've never understood what it is about that music that makes me get up and run away from it... the dances are infinitely Czech and they contain suppressed fire and a nostalgia for something that can never be brought back. There's the *Humoresque* and the symphonies, the cello concerto, fine, they're all masterpieces, but I love *Rusalka*, Dvořák's opera – for me the quintessence. If I had a son or daughter and if she was fifteen and I wanted to explain what the *Sezession* is, then *Rusalka* is its quintessence. In it you have the spirit of the age encapsulated to perfection, like Preisler's[187] picture of a girl day-

[187] Jan Preisler (1872–1918), leading Czech painter of the late nineteenth and early twentieth century, who combined elements of Naturalism, Symbolism, Impressionism and the *Sezession* (German, Austrian and Bohemian version of *Art Nouveau*).

dreaming. I am also affected by the knowledge that Dvořák, although, or maybe because, he qualified as a journeyman butcher, was capable of such humanity, such infinite artistic tenderness... as if there was a girl lurking in his soul, a young woman with one eye slightly displaced towards the Garden of Eden, like a rabbi's daughter gazing into the very heart of human infinity and human eternity... And he adored pigeons... Bedřich Smetana's *Triumphal Symphony*[188] – I don't know why, but I do a lot of flying and when the plane is still waiting for take-off with its engines at full throttle, the moment it lifts off I hear the *Triumphal Symphony* in the engines.

And what about operetta – one of the cornerstones of false illusion? It's had its own victims, suicidal serving-girls in Budapest and in Prague between the wars.

Oh yes. And I'm another of its victims. Mark you: if I were to choose what I might like to be in another life on earth, then not a writer. A singer in operetta. I mean, to me Lehár... He was past master. Same as with *The Bartered Bride*. Lehár can drive you to kitschy tears. Yet the tears are genuine. And then imagine that serving-girl, the ordinary workman and others. Operetta is the domain of ordinary folk. For them it isn't kitsch. It's the fulfilment of a world, something they would also like to be. At least a bit. Something they have never known, but would like to know. At least in the operetta. And they were always deeply affected, deeply; and it's no different today – take the content

---

[188] Written in 1853 in celebration of the marriage of Emperor Franz Josef.

of certain films, those with that same light touch you found in operettas, films like that one with Audrey Hepburn, *Roman Holiday*. It's a shocking film. Audrey Hepburn and Gregory Peck. A film operetta to take your breath away. If it had been me who wrote it, I'd swap it for all the *Closely Observed Trains* in the world. And *How to Steal a Million* with Peter O'Toole? The director, William Wyler, fascinates me. One great singer in Berlin in the 'Twenties, I think his name was Richard Tauber. He was taken to task for daring to sing *Lohengrin* when he also sang in Hungarian operettas, Lehár. And he told them: 'Begging your pardon: *Ich singe keine Operette, ich singe Lehár.*'

Do let me ask you to try to answer the question why it is possible that when a serving-girl heard Bach or Mozart she had no thought of suicide, but when she heard Lehár or Kálmán, [189] *she not only thought of it but she went ahead and committed it…*

It's something highly sentimental about man. When I was young, about twenty, twenty-five, there were servicemen at certain garrisons, especially lads from Slovakia, who would commit suicide just from hearing the song *Nedeľa smutná…* [190] They even banned the song because of the dozens of suicides. The music evoked a situation in the soldier-boy; it might look like a false spell, but the real spell, that sad Sunday, long Sunday, acted on the lad's mind, just as Chopin was

[189] Imre (Emmerich) Kálmán (1882–1953), Hungarian (or Austrian) composer, who lived abroad in Switzerland, France and the USA after 1938. His best-known operetta is *The Gipsy Princess*.
[190] 'Sad Sunday', a popular, melancholy Hungarian-Gipsy song, much performed by Slovak Roma bands.

affected. But the soldier couldn't express himself; Chopin could. His yearning for distant Poland, his native sod and everything that he had loved so much and left behind, he put all that into his music. But the serving-girls who saw Lehár or the soldier-boy who'd come from Slovakia and listened to *Nedeľa smutná* couldn't. All he could do was feel like not living. The music, that living song, that folk-song, that *Sad Sunday* evoked in him the insuperability of being here in Bohemia while in spirit he was elsewhere, so he jumped into the Vltava as if it were his Danube, or simply shot himself on duty, and so the song was banned. While operettas, as you can see, were never banned. But in the army, one precedent followed on the heels of another: playing that song was banned at garrisons everywhere.

I find it very surprising that if you were to be born again you would want to be not a writer, but an operetta singer.

Ah, Jára Pospíšil.[191] He was our darling. Jára Pospíšil, that's it. Jára... Let's not forget that even the great Bergman did a film of Lehár's *Merry Widow*.

But why are you so strongly drawn to operetta?

Because it fires the popular imagination. Or I might want to be a footballer. Same reason. Footballers get people, the masses, fired up, and everybody wants to be number one at something. I haven't been a writer, and when I've gone in for a spot of psychoanalytical

---

[191] Jára Pospíšil (1905–1979), hugely popular ragtime and operetta singer/actor, sometimes described as the Czechs' greatest-ever pop-star, idolised by women. His career peaked in the 1930s, but he continued recording into the 1960s, to a total of some 1,100 recorded songs.

daydreaming – *Tagesträume* – that run-of-the-mill psychopathology when you're lost in thought and get half an idea of what you'd like to be – I've had whole periods when I wanted to be Jára Pospíšil. And sing Lehár...

Have you also been an actor? Or an extra?
Well I was an extra at the S. K. Neumann Theatre. Back in Nymburk I once even played the lead, but very badly.

What in?
Goldoni's *Friends and Lovers*.[192] I played Don Juan, the lead in our performance, but I played him terribly – it just wasn't me. – But give me a shot at playing a footballer...

Being Puskás! I know! Hidegkuti. Pirouettes on a postage stamp!
No, I wanted to be Jirka Sobotka; Jirka had technique. Or Géza Kaloczaj, or Ferda Fascinek, or Horák of Slávia,[193] the one with the back-kick. I had such long dreams...

[192] 'Friends and Lovers' has been chosen here because of its obvious parallel with the Czech title given by Hrabal: *Milovat není jen mít rád* (To love is not just to like). *Friends and Lovers* is actually the English translation of *Il vero amico* (1750), in which the Don Juan character plays no part; it has recently been published together with *Don Juan* (1736) and *The Battlefield* (*La Guerra* [1760], trans. Robert David MacDonald, London, 1999). Apart from that publishing coincidence there is nothing to link the two plays, which are from distinct periods in Carlo Goldoni's (1707–93) career, nor is there any reason why *Don Juan* should not, like other Don Juan works, be given any other title in Czech than the protagonist's name. It would appear that, for whatever reason, the two plays had become confused in Hrabal's recollection.

[193] This recollection can be dated to the mid-1930s, when these heroes of Hrabal's, who were only one to three years older than he, were at the peak of

Do you still go to matches?

Yes, I do. Not often, but I do go, though not as a fan, just to watch.

Today it's Dukla v. Slávia.

Ah! And we're sitting here. Dukla v. Slávia, and today. I don't go to every match these days. And anyway, my main team was in Nymburk – Polaban Nymburk. They were in the league, my team. I was a supporter and travelling fan, and when they lost I was miserable. But you know how it is, without a crack in the brain you can't live... I expect that's why Bergman made *The Merry Widow*.

What are your favourite animals?

Cats. Cats. I merely put up with dogs, but if I want someone to lie down with me... I expect if I had a dog, it would probably be a dog. But in the small hours, when Pepito comes, jumps up on the bed to my wife and nuzzles up to her and looks into her eyes, still kind of full of fresh air and the scent of grass, at that time of the morning I sense and know that I'm both glad and awestruck, or I'm afraid of an event that I possess the key to. I know that the cat has kittens and six codes to go with them. One's for feed-

their careers with Prague's two leading football teams. Jiří (Jirka) Sobotka (1911–94), like Václav Horák (1912–2000), played for SK Slavia Praha; Géza Kaloczaj (1913–??) and Ferdinand (Ferda) Fascinek (1911–??) played for AC Sparta Praha, the latter specifically in 1934–37, but he is also remembered as an actor in the film *Naše jedenáctka* (Our eleven, a 1936 comedy, dir. Václav Binovec [1892–1976]). None of them were, apparently, thought of sufficient note to be indexed in Vol. 19 of Hrabal's Collected Works (Prague 1997), and I am grateful to Václav Boreček, archivist at Sparta for supplying many of these otherwise inaccessible data.

ing time, another for calling them to her, the third for a speedy disappearance, the fourth for playing dead, her fifth, affectionate code is for siesta-time, and the sixth is for bed-time. But I have no codes and no order, I'm alone, though not deserted, because I perceive everything that goes on around me like the task of being a mirror, a spherical advertising mirror crammed full of the extreme events of the everyday. For man, an animal is also light, you see. By taking everything so terribly earnestly and jumping with fright at the slightest thing I can casually change those miniatures at a moment's notice into nothing. In the end, everything trickles through my sieve of events, and all that remains is the sieve in my brain, the sieve in my heart. My love for everything that passes by me helps me experience infinity and eternity. Exuberance for the light that shines around my head, a nimbus. The core question: to be smitten by light, or not. My bone marrow and my brain fluoresce, I can tell from the way I walk, traipsing from place to place and always carrying with me that fixed point, that centre of light and the world... If the light leaves me or goes out for a moment – even if the sun is blazing away – I walk in darkness. If the wick of my oil lamp is turned right down, even if it's broad daylight, I grope with outstretched arms as if striding through a moonless night. As if I were a bird without wings. We're like animals driven into a corner; that is our sole certainty. Into a metaphysical corner. Our young thoughts are beaten to death. The essence of motherhood is the protection of one's young. And you know, if you do have animals, you have to feed them and you are their parent. You determine what they're going to eat and in a sense they are your children, or lovers.

And what about the doves of Prague?

They're just ornamental. Collared doves also arrived here from somewhere in the Balkans. They arrived suddenly. I read somewhere that half a million collared doves had been seen. What was only a caged curiosity when I was little has now arrived by the million. So here and there they even had to be destroyed. Whole treefuls of collared doves at once. People in charge of public health and hygiene claimed they'd brought certain infections. Or take another gift: in England all swans used to belong to the Queen. If anyone injured a swan, he got into trouble with the law. In this country we suddenly have – I don't know – a hundred thousand or half a million swans. Wherever you go where there's water there's simply an explosion of them, as scientists put it. A population explosion of swans. And that magnificent bird has now done Prague the honour of taking up residence, on our city ponds. So that royal bird is here, in a democratic republic, just flew in and now adds to the decor. Schoolchildren go and feed them, and when you see them there on the Vltava, or they do you the honour of flying over your head, two's enough, they have such mighty wings and give out such a noise as if there were a pump creaking in the distance. When a pair of swans fly over your head, you stand up and note the rhythmic working of their wings as they lever against the air, and their quills give out this strange creaking sound. And when a hundred flew over, it was almost like an eclipse... When you walk across Charles Bridge there's the gulls wheeling round the statues, giving everything around a new dimension. I reckon that both the pigeons and the collared doves, swans and gulls give Prague a whole extra dimension. What Calder[194] did, kinetic art, is represented and performed for us in Prague by those gulls, those collared doves, those pigeons. It's inseparable from Prague. Healthy, unhealthy, so what if it's unhealthy, but I feel honoured by them; as I am honoured, so too I reckon Prague is honoured; I'm honoured that I can dither about here, letting my eyes wheel around all those statues and all those towers and buildings and all the lovely people just like the gulls, the pigeons, the collared doves and the swans... Once, just above the Mánes,[195] where there's a weir on the river with a floodgate in the middle which the mighty current of the Vltava rolls through, I saw seven swans struggling valiantly against the current all the way to that very spot where the water gushing through the floodgate was stronger than even their best efforts... and only there and then, when there was no going further, did

[194] Alexander Calder (1898–1976), American sculptor and painter, the first exponent of kinetic art.
[195] A restaurant and assembly rooms, built in the Constructivist style (architect Otakar Novotný [1880–1959]) on one of the islands in the Vltava, close to the centre of Prague, and opened in 1930 for the Mánes Society of Artists (founded 1887), which became instrumental in introducing Prague to trends in contemporary art; also known for its Cubist ceiling painting by Emil Filla (1882–1953). Named after Josef Mánes (1820–71), the founder of Czech national painting and originator of the image of the Czech national hero from an idealised past. His father Antonín (1784–1843) is seen as the father of Czech landscape painting and his brother Quido (1828–80) was a painter of rural scenes.

the swans let up, hedonistically surrendering to the current and letting themselves be carried down that frizzy watery slope and through the swirls... all the way back to calm water... whereupon they lined up once more and hedonistically repeated the whole exercise.... and then again, and again... And I could see the swans' boundless excitement at their dangerous game with the counter-current from the flood-gate, the narrow throat in the weir through which the Vltava hurled its surging torrent... And at that instant I wished I could be with those swans at play and join in that apparently senseless, and yet so beautiful and blessèd game, because when I was a lad and there was June flooding on the Labe, when the water of the Vejrovka[196] rose by ten feet, I would dive into that furious, wildly rushing flow and let myself be borne along on the current until it carried me to calm water where I would paddle my way out and return upstream and hedonistically surrender once more to that whole dangerous, yet beautiful game – just like the seven swans playing in the floodgate on the Vltava... Here in Prague, standing on the bank near the Mánes, I experienced body and soul that wonderful sentence of Ladislav Klíma's... that animals are closer to God than man is, for them everything is a matter of course... ludibrionism is a divine game, a crazy and trifling and ignorant, and so beautiful, game. It's those pirouettes on a postage stamp at which Hidegkuti was such a genius... You know, Mr Szigeti, without a crack in the brain I can't live. But one ques-

---

[196] Officially Výrovka, a tributary of the Labe (Elbe), which it joins at Kosto-mlátky, a couple of miles west of Nymburk.

tion: Have you been swimming in the Malše[197] yet this year?

No, I haven't. But, Mr Hrabal, that new Turkish sultan must be a damn' good bloke. Thank you for granting me this interview. Thanks also for giving me an understanding of what Prague irony is...

---

[197] A repetition of the quotation from Hašek's *Schweik* (see p. 157); the Malše rises in Austria and flows into the Vltava near České Budějovice, capital of South Bohemia.

We began these conversations between Dunajská Streda and Prague and completed them at the Hungarian Cultural Centre in Prague; I answered Mr Szigeti's questions off the cuff, thinking originally that it would be easy, but after the seventh session I suddenly took fright and got nervous because I couldn't correct the tape recording. I was mortified in case I had said things that I didn't know enough about and so my answers might have been confused, ingenuous and therefore irresponsible... but Mr Szigeti had guts and may have been just starting out on his career as a journalist, and not only do I wish such people well, but I even offer them my talking head... And then, I am always curious about what will come next.

And so, one day, Mr Szigeti arrived from Dunajská Streda with a hundred and sixty pages of our conversation, which the girls back home had typed up for him from the tape... and I started reading it and that text was a mixture of Slovak and Czech and sort of Dadaistic sentences which made no sense at all... but I spent a fortnight reading... and when the conversation began to make me feel discordant, I sent the text back to him in the interest of my mental health for him to redo himself, and translate it into Czech... Thinking that Mr Szigeti would get cold feet and give up.

But Mr Szigeti did not give up and last year, just before Christmas, he brought me a hundred and forty pages and I discovered that the conversation was beginning to make sense, and that the surprise questions and my even more surprising responses were a prism whose glass facets cast a gently humorous glitter... And so I read it over and over again, cutting out the treatises on painters from Homework Assignments[198] *that Mr Szigeti had built into my replies – they did not match the colloquial flavour... here and there I used the collage technique to supplement some of my responses, and I designated the conversation an 'interview-novel'... But! As I was reading it through the next time, I began to smile: at the discovery that he had begun to relish the chaos the moment I referred to Hidegkuti's footwork, and taking a bird's eye view of the text I saw that the whole thing was like doing pirouettes on a postage stamp, and Hidegkuti's pirouettes overcame the semantic confusion not only of the questions, but also of my replies, that those same shortcomings in the dialogue were beginning to be fun for the reader, and that reading this conversation was like an antibiotic to cure convention and stereotyping... And so I gave the interview its title out of gratitude and respect to Mr Hidegkuti, who had the knack of so enhancing the game of football by his technical wizardry with the ball in a confined space that it was quite breathtaking, not only for the opposing team, but also for the spectators...*

In his steadfast dedication Mr Szigeti went on to add twenty questions on sex and the erotic and Central-European culture and politics... But, fortunately, I remembered Sigmund Freud, who once said... that we owe it to ourselves to be a little discrete... I remembered that Freud only declined to analyse his own dreams so as not to damage the family's good name... And so I declined to step onto the thin ice of Mr Szigeti's questions, since I too must observe a certain decorum and tact and not go letting any cats out of the bag as in a Catholic confessional... because beware, Mr Hrabal, beware! The hero of Hašek's novel, Schweik, is the coyest character in

---

[198] Hrabal's *Domácí úkoly z pilnosti* (1982).

the history of the world, and so too of the novel... It is my not so much belief as impression that this conversation, these Pirouettes on a Postage Stamp, are also borne along by the spirit of Prague irony, and that Jaroslav Hašek had so enlightened me that I have been able, by insertions and collage, to give the text a sense of playfulness...

B H *Kersko, 26ᵗʰ February 1986*

INDEX

(page-references in italics are to footnotes)

PIROUETTES ON A POSTAGE STAMP
                    BOHUMIL HRABAL

English translation by David Short
Published by Charles University
in Prague, Karolinum Press
Ovocný trh 3-5, 116 36 Praha 1
http://cupress.cuni.cz
Prague 2008
Vice-rector-editor
Prof. MhDr. Mojmír Horyna
Layout by Zdeněk Ziegler
Edited by Martin Janeček
Typeset by MU studio
Printed by Tiskárny Havlíčkův Brod, a.s.
First English edition

ISBN 978-80-246-1447-2